"If you're ▮▮▮▮▮ tonight, I ▮▮▮▮▮ do some su▮▮▮▮▮▮ ▮▮ ▮▮▮ ▮▮▮▮ ▮▮▮▮▮ ▮ go back there."

"Have you talked to them?" she asked.

"Not yet. I wanted to get you out safely and then find somewhere to talk about the situation," he said. "As long as we don't pick up a tail."

While Jude drove, he glanced at Kenley from the corner of his eye.

She was young, or at least younger than him. She was under five-four, and her body was lithe with curves in all the right places, which he'd learned when he put his arm around her waist to help her to the car. She had the perfect heart-shaped face, and her black hair bobbed at her shoulders and framed her cheeks to make her look younger than she certainly was. Her brown eyes were sharp and assessing, and her lips were naturally puckered.

When he first laid eyes on her, he immediately wondered what it would feel like to kiss them.

DARK WEB INVESTIGATION

KATIE METTNER

INTRIGUE

To the unseen and unsung heroes of the digital world
who protect us as we go about our daily lives.

**Harlequin®
INTRIGUE™**

ISBN-13: 978-1-335-45746-2

Dark Web Investigation

Copyright © 2025 by Katie Mettner

Harlequin Enterprises ULC
22 Adelaide St. West, 41st Floor
Toronto, Ontario M5H 4E3, Canada
www.Harlequin.com

Printed in Lithuania

MIX
Paper | Supporting responsible forestry
FSC® C021394

CAST OF CHARACTERS

Kenley Bates—Kenley, or Sickle as she's known on the dark web, is a cybersecurity expert by day. Come nighttime, she enters the underworld of the web, looking for justice for victims of corporate greed. Victims like her. When she sees something not meant for her eyes, she's sure her death warrant has just been signed.

Jude Mason—A cybersecurity expert recruited by Mina Jacobs of Secure One: Secure Watch Division. Once one of the military's top cybersecurity experts, he now works as a digital private investigator. He's lost enough people in life, and he's not looking to add to that scorecard, but a frantic call from Kenley has him racing to the rescue, where he finds himself tangled in an unseen web.

Savant (54V4N7)—A well-known bad apple on the dark web who has an IQ off the charts and a penchant for coding. He loves nothing more than to tangle with Kenley, but has he gone too far this time?

Spiderweb—An insentient AI program housed within a server farm in Iowa. Its true purpose is to become a weapon against the world. It's a threat to privacy and freedom worldwide if it can't be stopped.

Katie Mettner wears the title of "the only person to lose her leg after falling down the bunny hill" and loves decorating her prosthetic leg to fit the season. She lives in Northern Wisconsin with her own happily-ever-after and spends the day writing romantic stories with her sweet puppy by her side. Katie has an addiction to coffee and dachshunds and a lessening aversion to Pinterest—now that she's quit trying to make the things she pins.

Books by Katie Mettner

Harlequin Intrigue

Secure Watch

Dark Web Investigation

Secure One

Going Rogue in Red Rye County
The Perfect Witness
The Red River Slayer
The Silent Setup
The Masquerading Twin
Holiday Under Wraps

Visit the Author Profile page at Harlequin.com.

Chapter One

Kenley Bates tugged her stocking cap down lower over her ears and stepped inside the internet café; the sound of sirens and traffic dulled as the door closed behind her. Some might consider Metro Matrix a hangout for the dregs of Milwaukee, but no one better say that to Kenley's face. In her opinion, it was a term that implied everyone who lived in that part of the city was secondary to the rest of the city. Kenley had grown up there and knew the truth was something else entirely. Like any other neighborhood, the people did their best in a world where the deck was stacked against them. She should know—she'd lived it. Most turned their nose up when she mentioned the neighborhood she grew up in but living there had taught her something at an early age that too many people never learned: grab every opportunity that comes your way in life. Kenley worked hard to succeed and then pushed herself to take care of the people who helped her get there. It was important to her to stay true to who she was, no matter where she moved in life.

Knowing she had one way to help, she lived to learn and worked her fingers to the bone until she had a successful business and slept in an apartment overlooking the lake. That didn't make her any better than her friends at the Matrix. She lived in her clients' world so she could work for her people here. What her clients gave her, she could turn around and use to assist those truly in need. She was lucky that her natural-born talent could make a difference for those hurt and victimized by people who saw her clients as nothing more than cogs in a wheel.

Spotting an empty table in the far back corner of the café, she slid her backpack off and settled into the chair. Pretending to read the menu board above the small counter, she took a mental snapshot of the other users in the space. It was relatively empty for a Wednesday night, which she was glad about, but any one person could be the enemy she wasn't expecting. She opened her laptop and signed onto the Wi-Fi without looking away from the space around her.

Metro Matrix was her favorite place to set up shop when her white-hat hacking needed to turn a bit darker. The Matrix, as everyone called it, sold more than an internet connection to its customers. It also sold coffee, soda and snacks, but if you were looking for other services, you could get those, too. All you had to do was knock on the old wooden door three times and wait your turn.

Kenley had never knocked on the door. That wasn't why she took the bus ten miles one way to get here. At The Matrix, she could sit in the corner, run their Wi-Fi through her proxy scrambler and do what she needed to do on the darker side of the web without worrying that someone could track her. She also felt a tethered connection to her people when she sat at one of the tables. The friends and neighbors that she helped whenever she stepped over that white line in the sand. It was a place where she could relax in her work and get the answers someone needed to find justice.

At least that was how she usually felt, but not tonight. Tonight, she was nervous for a reason she couldn't define. High alert was an excellent way to describe it as she tugged her stocking cap down again to be sure her hair was still tucked under it. If she were honest with herself, she'd felt that way for several days now. It was like a hammer was about to fall, and she was in the way.

At thirty-one, some would say she was old enough to know better. Dabbling in the business of the dark web was risky business in and of itself, but Kenley had limited options if she wanted to help the people who had suffered too many atrocities in life. She knew what that felt like. Kenley's desire to fight for those without a voice—or maybe to fight for those drowned out by louder voices— came from life experience.

When she'd discovered in her senior year of high school that she had a natural talent for coding, she'd learned everything there was to know about it. Her quiet skills were loud when a job needed to be done. There were too many people without the skills to prove that they were being railroaded into silence by those with money and power, and Kenley refused to participate in their oppression. Not when she could stop it.

Did she feel dirty that her day job involved working for those who oppressed others? Yes, but it was the means to an end for her. While she spent her days writing code for corporations desperate to protect their business from ransomware and digital theft, she spent her nights sleuthing those same corporations for wrongdoing. She excelled at both jobs. She had more clients than time during the day, and while it afforded her a nice lifestyle, it didn't fulfill her the way her night job did. That was her true passion. Every time she found proof that could hold another big, lying corporation accountable for someone else's pain, it soothed the burn she had suffered. She'd once needed the same help, and when no one was there for her, she'd made it her life's mission to be the person others could turn to when all hope was lost.

After digging out her earbuds from her bag, she popped them in without connecting them to music. They helped her fit in, but music would prevent early warning of someone approaching unexpectedly. With her hands on the keyboard, she was ready to leave Kenley behind and become 51CKL3, her call name on most sites she frequented. Those were the sites where 51CKL3 found those needing help and where she could get a little justice for people who had suffered a tremendous loss.

Sickle was a fitting name for her, as her sole purpose was to cut companies off at the knees when they hurt the innocent. She glanced down at her right leg with a grim smile. She came by that name naturally. Unfortunately, after all these years, she still didn't have answers about her accident, but she refused to give up. Her friend had died for no other reason than greed, and Kenley was determined to prove it.

Her determination to find those answers was why she sat in The Matrix at 11:00 p.m. on a Wednesday in the middle of October. When she didn't have another client to take care of, she used her café time to find proof that her best friend had died due to negligence by the company that made the ATV.

She and Gabriella had been best friends their entire

childhood. Gabriella had been a beautiful girl with wavy red hair and freckles across the bridge of her nose. She was tall and loved to play basketball on the JV team. Kenley was the opposite, with long, straight black hair and a skin tone reflective of her Latina mother and Black father. Gabriella had moved in next door when the girls were only four. Since Gabby's mom was single, Kenley's mother had offered to watch Gabriella so her mom could work the night shift as a nurse. The girls shared Kenley's room five, sometimes six, nights a week growing up and were as close as sisters.

They were ready to start their sophomore year in high school when they'd made the fateful decision to take one last ride on Gabriella's ATV before school started the next day. A final goodbye to summer was said on the back of a four-wheeled machine barreling down a trail, which made them feel invincible. It was something they'd done hundreds of times before, but that day, Kenley had been tossed out of nowhere into the dirt, and her entire world had turned upside down.

Gabriella is dead.

It had been seventeen years, and she could still hear her mother say those three words. When they told her they'd amputated her right foot, it meant nothing to her. Her best friend was dead, and she didn't want to live if Gabriella wasn't by her side. Those were dark days. Days that Kenley tried to forget so she could focus on the one thing that got her through. Building the skills she'd need to prove that the parent company behind the ATV manufacturer was responsible for her best friend's death.

Using those coding skills, she had gotten justice for so many, but she still hadn't found proof that Staun Bril

Corporation knew the wheels of their Neo Chase ATVs could shear off at higher speeds. The lack of proof didn't mean they were innocent; it just meant she hadn't looked hard enough.

After checking into a few sites that used the power of the hive mind, she was ready to exit a chat room when she noticed a private message icon. Hope surged in her heart as she clicked it. While she waited for the message to load, she wondered if it was about her inquiries with the ATV manufacturer or a request for help from someone else looking for justice. When the page loaded, what filled the screen wasn't a request for help. It was a childish game that made her angry. She ground her teeth together as she dumped all the 0s and 1s into a text decoder and waited for the message to populate. She hated nothing more than dealing with an inexperienced child who thought secret decoding was necessary on the dark web. It wasn't, but for the sake of her quest, she'd decode the message on the off chance it was helpful. When the short sentence was revealed, she bit back a gasp.

Stop what you're doing before it's too late.

On instinct, Kenley glanced up and searched the nearly empty café. Goose bumps rose on her skin, and she swallowed nervously as her gaze darted around, taking in the other users who were either gaming or, in one case, watching banned anime. No one was paying her any attention, at least not in her physical landscape. Her digital landscape seemed to imply something else entirely.

Rather than buckle to the fear, she thrust her chest out and typed a message into a binary code translator before she copied the 0s and 1s into the text box and hit Send. If this jerk wanted to play, she'd play. It wasn't the first time she'd been challenged on the dark web, and it wouldn't be the last. It was important not to show weakness if she wanted to remain the hunter and not the hunted. It wasn't likely to come to anything more than a battle of wits from behind a screen. She left no identifying information behind, so outing 51CKL3 to the real world was impossible.

Kenley blew out a breath and shook out her shoulders. Maybe it was best to hang it up for the night. She was already jumpy, and that message didn't help matters, but her schedule didn't allow her to get back to The Matrix until the weekend, so she wanted to give the sender a chance to respond. Whoever was behind this was probably jockeying for position in the group—something Kenley couldn't care less about. She wasn't part of the group for the glory or the ego boost. She was there for information and justice. Nothing else.

Speaking of information, while she was waiting, she may as well access the Staun Bril Corporation files. If she were lucky, they'd have updated their research papers, and she'd find proof that they were aware of the axle problem on the older models of the ATV. That was all she needed. Proof that they *knew* the machines had a problem, but they sold them anyway.

Should her parents or Gabriella's mom have been the ones to bring a lawsuit against the ATV company? Yes, but there wasn't enough money for food and rent, much less lawyers. It had taken Kenley years to learn that others had suffered the same fate she had while driving the Neo Chase. Deaths. Amputations. Crush injuries. You name it, and it had been dealt out by the hands that steered the

Staun Bril Corporation. Kenley knew that they didn't care about people, only profits. If they cared about people, they would have recalled the machines the moment someone came forward with an injury. Not only did they not recall the machines, but they doubled down on advertising how safe they were and sold thousands more. In her opinion, that was the evil in this world.

The icon alert blinked that she had another message. Frowning, Kenley checked the time. It had only been four minutes. Whoever this was, they were waiting for her. She clicked on the red dot and waited for the 0s and 1s to load again. Once she had them decoded, her fingers faltered on the keyboard.

It doesn't matter who I am. I'm watching you, and you've been a very naughty girl.

Either this guy was a sicko, or he was somehow tracking her. She checked her proxy and shook her head in frustration. It wasn't possible. She never used the same IP twice, and using public Wi-Fi meant there was no way to home in on where or what she was doing online.

Kenley hated to do it, but she had little choice. She'd have to burn that forum and change her digital footprint again. Not that anyone could track her footprints, but changing her online name and persona was occasionally necessary to avoid showing up on radars like the one she'd found herself on. For all she knew, it was a cop behind that keyboard, and the last thing she would do was continue messaging until she walked into a trap.

Furiously clicking her mouse, she deleted everything she'd done on the forum as she backed out, finally deleting herself as a member. Then, she deleted the forum information from her server. Satisfied, she nodded before she signed back into the web. At least the person messaging her could no longer track her if they had figured out a way to do it through that forum. She knew it was impossible to be truly anonymous on the web. Still, without a username and the proxy scrambler mixing up her overseas locations, no one would know she was in a café in downtown Milwaukee, Wisconsin. At least they wouldn't know until she was long gone. As much as she hated to do it, this would be her last visit to The Matrix. Sometimes, you had to know when to fold a losing hand, and Kenley decided she'd just been dealt one.

There were always risks to playing on the internet this way, but the rewards usually outweighed them if you knew what you were doing, and she was confident that she did. She'd move around a bit and lurk through a few forums she never would have visited as 51CKL3, just in case someone was still looking for her. It was called a diversion digital footprint. Once she laid it down, she would stay off the dark web for a week. It was time to let everything cool off. If no one contacted her through the main web, she could reset all her black-hat profiles and start over.

Bored to death, she trolled through the general forums. Those forums eventually broke off into subjects that depended on your kink for that particular day. Kenley didn't have a kink unless you counted holding people responsible for harming others. She'd spent more than a few nights working with the police to shut down human trafficking sites. It would only be a matter of days before new ones popped back up, but their determination didn't faze her.

She kept reporting them because if someone made it difficult enough, maybe they'd give up.

Kenley let out a disenchanted snort. She knew better. That wasn't how human nature worked. Humans were predictable, even her, and rarely could you dissuade a human from doing something on the off chance they might get caught. Case in point—she typed an address into her browser. It was the digital locker where the Staun Bril Corporation held their manuals and research.

She knew the address by heart now, so when she hit Return, she grabbed her water bottle to drink while waiting for the page to load. What loaded wasn't what she was expecting, though. The background was black, with a white spider building a web. Slowly, the spider worked its way across the entire page, covering it in a web before scurrying back to the screen's center. This site was not the Staun Bril Corporation page. Kenley didn't know what it was, but her gut told her she had stumbled across something far more dangerous than ATV manuals. Before the page could disappear, she quickly wrote down the address in her notebook. While the spider continued to do nothing but stare at her, she compared the two lines of code. She had transposed several numbers. Quite unusual for her, but she was tired and working too fast, spooked by the messages she'd been sent.

The spider intrigued her. What would happen if she clicked on it? Like a moth to a flame, her finger hovered over the mouse until she took a deep breath and clicked. It took her to a new screen where tiny spiders with gigantic bulging eyes scurried across the page. Creepy didn't begin to describe it, but Kenley was hooked. She clicked on one of the spiders, and an image popped up. It was the view from a traffic camera. What was going on? After a couple more clicks, she realized each spider on the page went to a static public camera somewhere in America.

Undoubtedly, the dark web had weird games, but this didn't feel like a game. This was bigger. What was it? The next question was, who created it? She clicked on several more spiders, each showing her a view from a traffic or security camera. Leaning in, she realized some were not in the United States. The one she was looking at appeared to be somewhere in Japan.

Before Kenley could do anything, a new screen appeared with twice as many spiders waiting to scurry across the screen. She bit her lip and clicked one in the upper left corner. This time, webs shot from the spider with twelve smaller spiders at the end of each web. She clicked a smaller spider, and another traffic camera popped up. It showed her a familiar intersection. The next spider revealed a warehouse camera. Kenley leaned in as something tickled the back of her brain. She recognized the warehouse. Her eyes were glued to the screen, and she reached for her phone, where she dialed the only person who could help her now.

Chapter Two

Jude Mason was about to call it quits for the night. He'd had a long day of meetings with the team at Secure One and Secure Watch to integrate personal security client lists with their cyber clients. Secure One, a security company out of Northern Minnesota, had been integral in solving some rather harrowing crime cases over the previous few years and had seen the need for increasing cybersecurity. Since they had Mina Jacobs, who was one of the FBI's most talented hackers before she joined Secure One, as their lead cybersecurity expert, building a team around her to strengthen their offerings to clients made sense. Jude was ex-military, as were most people at Secure One, and he'd worked for Secure Watch remotely for almost two years. They kept him busy.

He'd known Mina since her days at the FBI when the military and defense department occasionally worked together. There wasn't much information Mina couldn't get her hands on when lives were on the line. That was the very reason Secure Watch began. Too many businesses and hospitals were falling victim to the evil hackers behind the keyboard. Those businesses needed a team that could stop attacks before they damaged their reputations or bankrupted them. Simply put, Secure One protected the exterior of the businesses while Mina and her crew protected their assets.

Jude had been working as a digital personal investigator for several years after leaving the military but didn't enjoy all the paperwork that came with the job. He'd much rather do the work and move on to the next client while someone else dealt with the business end, so when Mina called him unexpectedly a few years back, he couldn't say yes fast enough. Since he lived in Illinois, keeping him there to work remotely helped them cover the lower Midwest. It was a win-win as far as he was concerned. He could stay home and do the work he loved, but the albatross of paperwork and business advertising was gone.

His phone rang just as he reached for the lamp switch by the bed. With a sigh, he grabbed it and brought it to his ear. "Secure Watch."

"Delilah? It's Kenley." A woman whispered across the line, and while Jude didn't know anything about her, those three words were enough to tell him she was scared. "Wait, this isn't Delilah."

Jude chuckled, the sound low and not womanlike. "No, this isn't Delilah. You've got Jude Mason on the line."

"This is Delilah Hartman's number?" She asked the question as though she suddenly wasn't sure she'd dialed it correctly. "Or, uh, Delilah Porter?"

"It is, but she's on her honeymoon, so I'm taking her calls for Secure Watch while she's gone."

"How—how long will she be gone?" the woman asked, her nerves filling those few words.

"By the sound of your voice, longer than you want to wait. Maybe I can help you?"

"I just… I trust Delilah."

He sat up. Sleep wasn't happening tonight if this woman's voice was any indication. "I understand that, Kenley," he soothed, using the name she'd given him initially. "It's hard to trust someone you don't know on the other end of the line, right?"

"Yeah, I guess," she replied.

"I worked with Delilah in the military. That's why she gave me her phone while she was gone. She trusts me with her phone, which, she hoped, would show her clients that they can trust me too."

"That does make sense," she said, her voice softer the longer they spoke. "I'm a little freaked out and don't know what to do."

"Why don't you start by telling me what's happened?"

"I think I've come across something online that's… um…trouble." She cleared her throat as though she could banish the fear from her voice.

"Trouble for you?"

"Trouble for the entire world."

Those five words had Jude dropping his feet to the floor while he searched for his jeans. "Where are you?"

"At an internet café in Milwaukee," she said, as he flicked on speakerphone and pulled on a shirt. "I've been too afraid to leave."

"Is someone following you?"

Moving quickly, Jude tucked his wallet in his back pocket, tied on his shoes and started to gather his equipment.

"Digitally? Possibly."

"What about physically?"

"Hard to say," she said, and he could tell she was hedging. "I don't think so, but after what I found, I can't say that for sure."

"Give me your current address," he said, grabbing his other phone and typing in the address she rattled off. To say it was in a less-than-safe neighborhood of Milwaukee was being kind. That neighborhood was rough when the sun was out, but walking through it as a single woman at midnight was like playing Russian roulette.

"Is the café open all night?" he asked, pocketing his other phone and keys before he picked up his bags and walked out of the house, locking the door behind him.

"Yes, but I don't know how long I should stay here."

"You're going to stay there another hour and thirty-six minutes," he said, slamming the back door to his SUV closed after he tossed in his bags. "That's how far away I am. Traffic should be light. Hopefully, I can make up some time on the interstate."

"You're coming? Here?"

"You called Delilah for help, right?" he asked, firing up his vehicle and turning on the heater. It may only be October, but at 1:00 a.m., the night had a chill about it.

"Yes, but Delilah is my friend. I'm not sure I can afford to employ Secure Watch to help me with this."

"Don't worry about that right now," he said, the fear in the woman's voice hitting him straight in the gut. As an ex-military man, a woman in need activated his protective side, but there was something different about this woman. He could hear the thread of fear in her voice, but he could also hear something else. Determination? Strength? Both? She needed help, but she didn't need saving. He would do well to remember that when he approached her. "I'll reach out to Secure Watch and let them know I'm just getting you home safely."

Her laughter was relaxed for the first time since he'd answered, so he smiled, relieved that some of the fear had left her voice, if only for a few moments. "What happens if it's more than a ride home?"

"We'll cross that bridge when we get there," he assured her. "While I drive, why don't you tell me what's happened?"

"No," she whispered, her voice low and the fear back in full force. "No. Not a good idea. Terrible idea. Everything has ears, Jude. You know this."

"Okay, you're right. Hang in there. I'm on my way. I don't want you to hang up, but I know you're scared, so how about if we listen to music together?"

"I thought you had to call Secure Watch?"

"That can wait," he assured her, reaching for the radio. "What kind of music do you like? Please tell me you aren't a metalhead."

She laughed again, and while it wasn't as relaxed as before, it wasn't forced either. "No, I'm not a metalhead. My dad always said I was born in the wrong decade regarding my taste in music. My top three are Ella Fitzgerald, Count Basie and Nat King Cole."

"A jazz lover? I can appreciate that," he said, tuning the radio to 90.9 FM. A soft, plaintive piano solo filled the car.

"Billie Holiday," she said, bringing a smile to his face as he merged onto I-94 and pushed the speedometer to 75. She was clearly frightened, and Jude didn't want to dawdle and risk her leaving the café before he got there. He'd keep her talking about anything and everything so she didn't register the passage of time. He had no idea what Kenley had gotten herself into, but he did know one thing: walking out the door of that internet café might put her life at risk, and he couldn't have the death of anyone else on his conscience, no matter the cost to himself.

WHAT WAS SHE DOING?

Kenley asked herself that question every minute she stayed on the line with Jude. 51CKL3 didn't ask for help. She'd learned how to help herself. Yet, here she was, letting Jude Mason calm her down with jazz history and random stories about his days as a private investigator. She'd shut down her equipment and stowed it in her backpack, but she couldn't find the courage to hang up the phone and leave the café. She was spooked by the messages, but the program she'd accidentally found her way into terrified her. Were they connected? They couldn't be, right? There was no way anyone could predict she would reverse two numbers in a line of code to happen upon their site. It had to be a coincidence. A coincidence that could be deadly if what she saw on that warehouse camera was any indication.

Before she closed out of the system, she'd copied as much information as she could about the Spiderweb program. She'd planned on having Delilah help her map the code once she got back into it, but that was a nonstarter if she was on her honeymoon. Did she trust Secure Watch, the company Delilah now worked for? She did. Explicitly. She needed no more proof that they were on the up-and-up than knowing Delilah worked for them. Adding to their reputation were all the women they'd saved from a trafficking ring, and by catching a serial killer. If Jude Mason worked for them, she didn't doubt that he was the best of the best, too. That wasn't what she was afraid of. She was afraid of dragging someone else into this until they were in over their heads.

Delilah was a master hacker like herself, so Kenley wasn't worried about calling her for help, but she had no idea what kind of skills Jude Mason had. Asking on an open line that anyone could be tapped into was also too big a risk. Since no one had come for her, chances were good no one else was listening in, but it was still better to ask these questions face-to-face.

"Are you still there, Kenley?" Jude asked, his words sharp. They snapped her back to reality, and she nodded as she spoke.

"Yes, yes, sorry, I was getting my things together. Where are you?" Was she seriously considering getting into a car with this guy? The better question was, did she have a choice? In her opinion, considering the situation, she didn't. If he could get her out of this café safely, she could reassess and make a plan. Knowing Delilah had trusted Jude with her phone told Kenley he was trustworthy.

"I'm pulling into the neighborhood now. Do not come out. I'll park and come to you."

"That won't be easy," Kenley said, eyeing the street through the front windows. "It's not exactly paid parking down here."

"I've double-parked a Humvee in Kabul. I think I can handle downtown Milwaukee."

So, he *was* ex-military. That made sense, considering how he jumped into battle with little information. She was already knee-deep in this adventure with him; she may as well play it out.

"I'll be ready," she said, sliding her backpack over her shoulders. "Should I hang up?"

"Yes, I'm pulling up now," he answered. "Toyota 4Runner."

After stowing her phone in her pocket, she casually walked toward the front of the café as if it were any other night. Her gaze was glued to the SUV as a man emerged. Immediately, she assigned tall and dark to the man. He was nearly a foot taller than her five feet, and his dark hair was still cut high and tight. He turned, and she added handsome to her description. It would have been hard not to notice his chiseled jawline accentuated by a goatee, making her wonder what it would feel like brushing against her skin.

Whoa, girl, back up the lustometer, she scolded herself. *He's here to help you, not kiss you.*

A smile tipped her lips at the thought, and as he pulled open the door to the café, she noticed how his muscles bulged under his light jacket. He kept up his military fitness; there was no question.

His gaze locked with hers, and that was when she took in everything else about him in a heartbeat. Hidden behind a pair of silver spectacles were eyes the shade of peridot. She'd heard that green eyes were the rarest color in the world. That made her wonder if the man before her, who assessed the entire café as he waited for her to walk toward him, was equally as rare. When she got closer, she noticed his goatee was dotted with white hair, attesting to his maturity rather than vanity. He tugged her close to his side as soon as she was within reach.

"Head down, straight to the car," he whispered, practically carrying her around the parked car's bumper to get to his. He opened the door for her and took her backpack while she climbed in. He deposited the bag at her feet, closed her door and drove away before she got her seat belt buckled. This man meant business. When she glanced at him, his determination told her she no longer needed to be scared.

Her only worry was that the feeling wouldn't last for long.

Chapter Three

"I'm Jude, by the way," he said, extending his hand for her to shake. The woman in his passenger seat seemed all shaken up and needed a friendly face, even if it was a face she'd never seen before. "I've worked with Delilah on and off for years, first in the service and now with Secure Watch."

She slipped her hand into his and gave it a firm shake, something he wasn't expecting, considering her petite frame. He also didn't expect to feel the snick of connection the moment their skin touched.

"It's nice to meet you, Jude. I'm Kenley Bates. I'm sorry for messing up your plans for the night. I forgot Delilah was on her honeymoon."

"Did you watch the ceremony?" he asked, hoping the small talk would help them relax.

"I did. Saying your vows as the sun sets over Lake Superior might be the most romantic thing I've ever seen."

"I couldn't agree more. I'm just glad they figured out a way to do it that allowed everyone to be part of the wedding without being there in person. That island was special for them?"

"Oh, yeah," she agreed with a nod of her head. "They spent a summer on Madeline Island after being discharged from the army. That was before Delilah had to go on the run to protect Lucas. I'm glad they found their way back to each other. I can't say their honeymoon is super convenient for me, though." The self-deprecating laugh she gave at the end made him smile.

"I promise we will help you out of this jam. Like I said, I worked with Delilah in the service, so I was all in when Mina approached me about working at Secure Watch on her recommendation. Their new cyber division already has more clients than they can handle."

"What branch of the military were you in?" she asked.

"Army, just like the rest of Secure One."

"It seems to be a theme for them, which is understandable, considering Cal feels responsible for everyone getting hurt that day in the war. At least that's the vibe I got from Delilah."

"He did, in the beginning, but with time and love from his wife, Marlise, he sees that he had no better chance of stopping that car bomb than any of the other guys there that day. That's the thing about war. Even if you survive, you don't survive. The person you were before you went into battle does not come back out from it. You're changed on a cellular level, and it takes a long time to accept that."

"Have you?" she asked, her gaze heating his cheek from the intensity of it.

"I'm different," he said tersely. "I went to war from the comfort of a desk chair. I don't get to call myself a warrior like they do."

"Did you see things you wished you'd never seen?"

He nodded rather than answer while he kept his eyes peeled to the rearview mirror for a tail. "Do those things ever wake you up in a cold sweat at night until you remember you're home in bed?" Again, it was easier to nod in acknowledgment than to speak. "Sounds to me like you were also changed on a cellular level. Maybe not the same way as those physically injured in war, but we all know the mind is just as easy to damage as limbs."

"Probably easier," he agreed with a sigh. "That's why Cal always looks for veterans to hire when positions open. There aren't many of us who do this kind of work, so Mina has convinced him we will have to hire from the civilian population. Cal agreed as long as she prioritized people with disabilities, which is a much deeper well to drink from."

"I'm not surprised," she said with a chuckle. "Both about your new well and how many clients you have clamoring for help. I run my own business securing websites from the threat of bricking and ransomware and have more calls than time."

"Secure Watch has the same problem, but then add in the clients who need help when their system is bricked, and they've had to grow faster than they predicted." His gaze darted to the rearview mirror. "No tail yet."

"That's good, right?" she asked, as though he knew the correct answer.

"As long as it stays that way," he agreed. "I don't think returning to your place is safe, though."

"But we have to," she said, slightly frantic. "I need my things."

"I'll stop at a Target once we hit Chicago," he said, signaling left onto the interstate. "That's a safer idea."

"The things I need you can't get at Target," she said as she slowly lifted her right leg and then pulled her pants up.

One fast glance was all he needed. "You're an amputee?"

"Symes," she agreed. "You could say I'm part of your well." He couldn't stop the smile that lifted his lips. "But I'll need my supplies." Before she could say more, she held up a finger. "Wait, if you aren't taking me to my place, where are you taking me?"

"I don't know, but if you're alarmed by what happened tonight, I think we better have Secure One do some surveillance on your place before you go back there."

"Have you talked to them?"

"Not yet. I wanted to get you out safely and then find somewhere to talk openly about the situation. That was going to be my place. I wanted to be home before sunrise but wasn't planning on another stop."

"It's on the way," she promised. "I can be in and out in under five minutes. We'll still make Chicago long before the sun comes up."

"As long as we don't pick up a tail," he said, and she nodded, giving him the address.

While he drove, he glanced at Kenley from the corner of his eye. She was young, or at least younger than him. She was under five-four, and her body was lithe with curves in all the right places, which he'd learned when he put his arm around her waist to help her to the car. She had the perfect heart-shaped face, and her black hair bobbed at her shoulders and framed her cheeks to make her look younger than she certainly was. Her brown eyes were sharp and assessing, and her lips were naturally plump. When he first laid eyes on her, he'd licked his own, his mind immediately wondering what it would feel like to kiss them.

Jude shook his head with a huff and turned right off the interstate, following her directions. Another truck followed them off the exit, and he went on full alert, pushing thoughts of kissing Kenley out of his mind as he committed to memory everything about the truck behind them.

"What's the matter?" she asked, glancing at him as he sped up for a light about to change to red.

"Maybe nothing," he said between clenched teeth. He ran the yellow, and even though it turned red halfway through, the truck stayed on his bumper. "Hell," he groaned. Bright headlights filled his mirrors, preventing him from seeing the driver.

"That truck is following us?" she asked, and he reached out and stopped her from turning around. His hand tingled where their skin connected, but he pushed the reaction aside.

"Yes, but don't look behind you. I don't want them to confirm it's you in the car. We can't go to your house now. They'll know for certain it's you if we do."

"Where are we going, then?"

"I'm going to get us back on the interstate," he said, noticing an entrance ramp ahead.

"We can't go to your place either, then. They'll know you're helping me."

"Well, they already know that, but I'd prefer that whoever they are, they don't know where I live. I'm going to head north until we lose them."

"Do you think we can?"

"Hang on tight," he said with a wink and then yanked the wheel to the right, jumping over the low curb of the turn lane and rocketing down the entrance ramp. The truck overshot and kept going, exactly what he had hoped for. "They missed the turn. They'll find us again, but we've got time to put distance between us."

"Maybe we should get off the interstate?" she asked as he pushed the SUV to eighty. "If they can't find us, they can't follow us."

She was right. It was hard to hide out here when the road was deserted, and they had at most ten minutes before the truck caught up to them.

"That's assuming they were following us," he said, rubbing his chin for a few seconds. "It could have been a coincidence."

"It didn't feel that way to me," she said. "I was watching them in the side mirror. There was no one near us, and then suddenly, that truck was right behind us, and they kept pace."

"That's what my gut says, too," he finally agreed, reading the signs ahead of them. Chances were, they'd encounter the truck after the next exit if he didn't get off the interstate now. If he got off here, he could take the back roads home. It would take longer, but it gave him more options should they pick up another tail. "I don't know what you got yourself into, Kenley Bates, but getting you back out of it will be more involved than I initially thought."

"And you haven't even seen the tip of the iceberg," she muttered.

"Hang on," he warned, and she grabbed the door handle as he turned the wheel to the left, coasted up the ramp, turned right, and then took a two-lane road that was pitch-black on this moonless October night.

As the vehicle rocketed down the road, he couldn't help but think he was the one who needed to hang on now that Kenley Bates was in his passenger seat.

KENLEY WOKE WITH a start, the sun rising over the horizon as the truck slowed for a light. She glanced around frantically until she laid eyes on the man next to her, and it all came flooding back: the café, the desperate call, and the truck that followed them.

"Morning, sleepyhead," he said as he turned right at the light.

"How long have I been out?" she asked, rubbing her face to ensure she wasn't drooling. There was nothing as embarrassing as being in a car with a cute guy and having drool stains on your face. No drool was noticed, so she let out a sigh of relief.

"Not long," he answered. "Only about twenty minutes. You needed it, and all was quiet. We're almost at my place. We can't stay there long, though."

"I figured," she agreed. "They probably got your plate and already know where you live."

"Not yet, but once they break through the information for several shell corporations and businesses that don't exist, they'll know where I live."

"Paranoid much?" she asked, a brow raised.

"By the looks of it, not nearly enough," he answered, briefly lowering a brow at her. "We're a few blocks away. First, I'll do some recon of the streets surrounding the house. I have to be sure no one is waiting in a parked car for us."

"How would you know? Streets in the city are lined with cars."

"Not so much in my neighborhood," he said, his tone chipper as they turned down a street lined with landscaped lawns and perfectly clipped trees. Neat-as-a-pin homes were circled with white picket fences. The only thing missing were the 2.5 kids and the dog. Then again, maybe they were inside getting ready for another day in suburbia.

Kenley whistled as they drove down street after street

with houses that all looked identical. "I stand corrected. We don't have much in common."

She noticed his eyes never left the road when he spoke. "Never assume that what you see is what you get, Kenley."

That was fair. It was certainly the case with her. When people met her now, they never imagined that she'd grown up in the inner city. She might not know Jude well, but she didn't see him living in a home like this. He gave off more log cabin vibes than suburbia vibes.

"I don't live here by choice but because it offers safety in numbers. If I had my druthers, I'd live in a cabin in the woods."

Kenley's laughter filled the car. "It's like you can read my mind."

"Your face is rather—" he motioned in the air with his hand "—expressive."

"I've heard that before," she conceded, biting back a smile as he slowed for a driveway. His house was smack-dab in the middle of the block.

"The neighbors are close enough to see anyone trying to break in and to hear my alarm system," he explained, pulling the SUV into the garage. The door slid closed behind them, and he finally let go of his death grip on the wheel. "Everything looked quiet, but we aren't going to push our luck. We'll take ten minutes to get in touch with Secure Watch, grab some extra equipment I didn't know I'd need, and get back on the road."

"Is it safe to drive this again?" she asked when he opened her door.

"Nope. We'll have to take a short walk to pick up a new one. Can you walk half a mile or so?"

"I can walk that far without my prosthesis," she answered. "I won't slow you down."

He closed the door quietly and motioned for her to stay up against the garage wall while he unlocked the door. He made the checking sign with his fingers to his eyes, and she nodded, allowing him to sweep the home. Chances were good that no one had figured out who he was yet, but better safe than sorry. She'd used a burner to call him, and he was smart enough to hide his vehicle registration under a few red herrings, which not everyone thought of when in this business. They couldn't waste time, though. She didn't know who was behind the threats or the Spiderweb site, and until she did, they had to stay on their toes. That was easier said than done when they were both exhausted.

"All clear," he called, and she walked into the house, closing and locking the door behind her.

From her vantage point in the kitchen, Kenley watched him scurry around what should be the living room. Instead of a cozy vibe, it had blackout shades on both windows and enough computer equipment to make her jealous.

"Holy schnikes." She whistled as she walked into his space, her eyes trying to take it all in simultaneously. "You know how to turn a girl on."

He paused in his packing and raised a brow. "Like what you see, darling?" His smirk told her he was joking as she ran a finger across a top-of-the-line server. "Orgasm by computer wasn't what I was going for, but go ahead, I'll wait." He crossed his arms over his chest and leaned back on the table to emphasize his point.

"Har-har," she said, sticking her tongue out at the man

she should not be discussing orgasms of any kind with. "You're hilarious. Not. Did you get what you need?"

"Almost," he answered, stuffing a few more things in a bag. "Now it's time to meet Mina Jacobs. She could be the one to save your life."

She would bet anything the man doing the talking was in the running for that title, too, but having an FBI hacker on her team wasn't nothing. Knowing their time was short, all Kenley could think was Delilah had done her a solid by flying off to Hawaii for her honeymoon and leaving Jude Mason in charge of her phone.

Chapter Four

"Do you have any powder?" Kenley asked as he was packing up his equipment.

He paused and turned to her. "What kind of powder?"

"Anything that absorbs sweat would work."

He pointed down the hall to her left. "The third door on the right is the bathroom. There should be some Anti Monkey Butt Powder in the cabinet on the top right shelf. I use it for running."

"You're my hero, Jude Mason," she said in her best Ferris Bueller voice. "Give me five, and I'll be ready to connect with Mina."

"Throw the bottle in your bag," he said as she headed down the hallway. "You might need it."

He was right. She probably would need it if she couldn't return to her place sooner rather than later. Considering the situation, that didn't look promising. She passed a bedroom and paused. It was a guest room, but that wasn't what caught her eye. Through the window, she swore the truck from earlier had just cruised past it. It was an old single-cab truck with thick metal mirrors and strong window tinting. She could count three people inside the vehicle, and while it had been too dark last night, today she noted they were all male.

She shook her head and walked into the bathroom, confident it couldn't be the same truck. Not only was it too soon for them to have found Jude's place, but there were a lot of old white trucks on the road. She couldn't start tilting at windmills every time she saw one. After a quick search for the powder, she found it exactly where he said it would be. Thankfully, the calamine in the powder would keep her limb from itching and absorb the sweat that was to come from walking to his bug-out car.

She quickly pulled the Velcro strips off that held the plate on the back of her prosthesis and pulled her limb from it. After she rolled the special liner sock off, she washed and dried it before covering her limb in powder. The liner sock was a new addition to her prosthesis. Her limb had slowly atrophied to the point that every time her shinbone bumped up against the carbon fiber prosthesis, she was miserable. They'd remedied it using a five-ply sock with an internal gel liner. It took care of the pain but caused a sweating problem she had never had before. At least there were products to help with the sweating issue. It was the lesser of two evils because walking was hard when your leg hurt with every step.

After her leg was back in the prosthesis and the plate was secure again, she washed up and grabbed the powder before returning to the living room. She paused again in the guest room doorway, the hair up on the back of her neck. Stepping into the room, she walked to the window and stood to the side, dropping lower when she noticed the same pickup drive past the house again. Once it passed the room, she darted into the hallway and entered the living room.

"The truck." The two words came out winded but precise.

Jude froze with his finger on a button of some device. "*The* truck?" Her nod had him grabbing the device and sticking that in his bag, too.

"I've seen it twice now. It must be going around the block waiting for us to leave."

"That's going to make leaving a bit more complicated," he said, hoisting the bag over his back. "The fence will buy us time to avoid detection, but eventually, we'll have to step into the open."

"Your backyard has a fence?"

"Yes," he said, motioning her toward the back door again. "Stay low to avoid the kitchen window."

Kenley ducked and followed him to the door, where a half wall gave them cover from the window while he unlocked it.

"It's a tall wooden fence I had put up. You'll understand why when I show you where my surveillance car is. Follow me." With her nod, they left the garage and hurried through the backyard. Kenley listened for tires on the pavement but heard nothing before they reached the end of the fence.

"Do we go over?" she asked in a whisper.

He shook his head and knelt, clicking a button on the bottom of one of the boards, and then a gate swung open.

"I'd say paranoid, but I'm too thankful not to have to scale that fence," she whispered after he cleared the back side and motioned her forward.

"How did they find us so quickly?" he wondered between clenched teeth.

"I wish I could tell you, but I can't. All I know is it was the same truck," she said, her words nothing more than a whisper on the wind. "I saw it when I walked into the

bathroom and again on the way out. I haven't heard a vehicle since, so maybe I had it all wrong?"

"No one should have found us this quickly," he muttered as they dipped into the pine forest that edged the
neighborhood. With any luck, they'd escape while the
truck was doing another round of surveillance.

Kenley could tell Jude was frustrated. She didn't know
him that well yet, but his body language told her that
much. He was also confused but working hard to control
his emotions so she didn't feed off them. Unfortunately,
he wore them like a button-up shirt. Cool heads had to
prevail if they were to get out of this town before the truck
showed up again.

"Mina's an amputee, too," he said as though it would
help her connect with someone she had never met or, at
the very least, distract her.

"Bet she didn't kill her best friend to become one,"
she muttered.

"That's oddly pointed, but no, she was beaten by a
woman who discovered she was an undercover FBI agent
trying to take down her sex trafficking ring. Roman said
it was gnarly."

"Who's Roman?"

"Mina's husband. He was her partner in the FBI. Now
he works for Secure One. He's Cal's foster brother, and
they served together in the army."

"I'm sorry we didn't get to call her before we left," she
said, as though it was her fault that some maniac in a truck
was hunting her. Then again, maybe it was her fault. She
probably should remember she might have started this
whole chain reaction.

"I brought my equipment with me, and once we get

somewhere safe, we'll call in. Since it's early, no one will expect me to check in until later. If nothing else, the early hour of the morning bought us time. That said, it's almost seven thirty a.m., and the sun is out, leaving us vulnerable to whoever is searching for us."

"Hold up. I'm afraid we aren't going anywhere."

JUDE PEEKED OUT around the tree until he caught a glimpse of what she had seen.

"There," she whispered, pointing to his left.

Relief filled him. "That's just Boone." He pulled her out from behind the tree and headed for the edge of the forest that butted up to the community soccer field. "He's Mr. Hamel's Maine coon. Boone has been mistaken for a bobcat more than once. He's on the prowl."

"Mr. Hamel will find himself short a kitty if he keeps letting him roam. I've never seen a cat that big. In a neighborhood like this, someone will shoot first and ask questions later."

"Can't disagree," he said, pushing her harder to finish the walk to the garage where he kept his surveillance car. The last thing he wanted was someone to report them to the cops for lurking. He would have done it at a jog but suspected her prosthesis wouldn't allow it. Her entire calf was encased in a carbon fiber socket with the prosthetic foot attached so close to the ground that there was very little clearance for any ankle. Her gait was smooth, but running wasn't easy for her, which he'd learned when he pushed her too hard as they left the house. She was quick on it, but she'd nearly fallen in their haste, and he didn't want her to get hurt. "The garages are coming up on your right," he said, pointing them out through the branches.

"Once we leave the trees, we have a lot of open space to cover until we reach them." The hulking buildings he pointed out housed everything from cars to boats to RVs.

"First, if we make it there undetected, which I question, where will we go? If the guys from last night are in that truck, they'll follow us."

"Ultimately, I want to get to Secure Watch."

"Isn't that six or seven hours away?"

"Just about," he agreed, "but when it comes to the danger we're dealing with, at least the little bit you told me, the only safe place is Secure Watch. They have security you aren't going to find anywhere outside of a military base or Taylor Swift's house."

Her snort was audible over the sound of the birds chirping, and it brought a smile to his lips. She enjoyed snark, and he could appreciate that in a woman. He'd just be happy if she bought his story about Secure Watch. That was all it was, though. There wasn't a chance in hell he would bring any of this to their doorstep.

"I just don't think it's smart to drag anyone else into this fiasco," she explained as they prepared to leave the trees and head to the giant metal warehouse. The building was divided into individual climate-controlled garage stalls, and everyone had separate garage doors and openers. It was the perfect place to store his Jeep when he didn't need it for work, but its central location hindered this situation.

"Wait," she said, grabbing his jacket sleeve. "On the left side of the street, what do you see?"

His gaze traveled down the street that led from the dead end. There sat a familiar truck with its nose pointing out.

"They're waiting for us to leave so they can follow

us rather than hunt us down and raise suspicion in the neighborhood. What have you gotten yourself involved in, Kenley?" he asked, his gaze darting to her for a heartbeat. "There's no way they should know who I am or where I live yet."

"Let's just say the people I associate with can do much more than break through a couple of LLCs. The ones I don't associate with but who know my name can do even more."

"Do you happen to know which one we're dealing with here?" he asked, trying to decide on their next move.

"Nope," she said, popping the *p*. "But the fact they're waiting to follow us rather than having already killed us is encouraging."

"Well, some good news for once," he said, a shudder racking him as he pulled his Sig from his holster. "It's time to load up the Jeep and get out of town."

"How will we do that when they're blocking our only way out?"

"My surveillance vehicle is an off-road Jeep for a reason. The garage butts up to a trail for ATVs."

"You've thought of everything, Mr. Mason," she whispered. "Except how we're going to get out unheard."

He had thought about that and hadn't found a good answer yet. The Jeep was new and quiet, but if they heard a garage door or an engine catch, they would know it was them.

"We'll address that once we make it across this open space. They'll be watching their rearview, but I don't see any other option here."

"I think the answer is obvious, Jude. The Jeep is not worth the risk."

"Why do I hate it so much that you're right?"

"Probably because it limits our options," she answered with a tip of her lips. "Should we go back for the truck?"

His sigh was heavy when he turned to her and took her shoulders. "No, the truck has already been tagged. I'm afraid our walk will be long if we decide to abandon the Jeep."

"I'll keep up," she promised, shifting the pack's weight on her back.

His nod came with a gentle smile. "I know you will. If we can put some distance between us and the three guys in the truck, we can send an SOS to Secure Watch. When that comes in, they'll know I'm in trouble without an actual call."

"Do it now," she urged, her gaze glued to the truck with three heads visible through the back window.

"It's smarter to wait until we're somewhere they can pick us up without getting tagged."

"That's the frustrating part," she said, shaking her head. "I don't understand how they tagged me to begin with, Jude. My machines are clean. So is my phone."

His gaze traveled the length of her, and he froze for a moment before he reached into his bag and pulled out his wireless signal wand. "Let's make sure before we go any further."

He swept the wand over and around her backpack several times before she grabbed it and held it still. "What are you doing? I'm talking about a program used to track devices."

"I know," he said with a wink. "But they have small trackers, so you might not notice if someone dropped one in your bag."

"I would know if there was a tracker in my bag. I empty it every time I get home."

"Do you shake it out too?"

Her eye roll was enough of an answer. She released the wand, and he checked the seams at the bottom of the bag before running the wand over her coat pockets. "You're clean. I don't understand it."

"I told you that," she said as he dropped the wand to his side. When it went off, he jerked it back to center. "Was that you?"

"It was something," he agreed, running the wand back over his shoes and pockets, but this time, it didn't sound, so he ran it across the ground, wondering if something in the soil was giving them a false positive. He was ready to give up when she moved her foot, and the wand beeped. He glanced up at her and, this time, ran the wand over her prosthesis, slowly moving it down to her shoe, where the wand beeped again. "Is that even possible?" he asked as he stood and stowed the wand in his bag again.

"The foot shell is open, but it would have to be so small, Jude."

"They make small trackers now. Here," he said, taking off his coat and spreading it out on the ground, motioning for her to sit.

The look she gave him was uncertain, but she sat, pulled her shoe off, and then worked at the rubber shell until it popped off the metal foot. Out fell a small round tracker that lay on the ground like a shining specimen of deceit.

"Don't touch it," he said, holding her hand back from picking it up.

"We should look at it. Maybe it will tell us who put it there."

"It won't," Jude assured her, working the rubber shell back over her prosthetic foot once he'd scanned her again to be sure she was clear. "It's a simple one you can buy on the internet in a ten-pack. If I had to guess, they've got one stuck somewhere in your car, too. I'm honestly surprised they didn't go for your bag, but the foot was brilliant. You're never without it."

"Not untrue, but when?" she asked, her confusion real as he tied on her shoe.

"It had to be somewhat recent since the battery is still working on it. We don't have time to worry about that right now, though," he said, helping her up. He shouldered his coat and then his bag. "They're sitting there waiting because the tracker tells them we're moving in their direction, so let's go somewhere else. The faster we get away from it, the bigger head start we get on them. It won't take long before they figure out we found it and left it behind. We'll go right and follow the trees to where they end at the creek. We'll cross there and hike to the next town. We can make decisions once we're clear of the tracker."

Kenley opened her mouth, and he thought she was going to argue, but after staring at him for two beats, she turned to her right and took off through the trees.

Chapter Five

The terrain was rugged, but Kenley refused to ask Jude to slow down or for a break. She would keep pace with him if it killed her. They were in this mess because of her, so she would do anything to keep up with the guy trying to save her life. He was giving her time to figure out what was happening. She had no proof that someone wanted her dead, but she also didn't think the guys in the truck just wanted to talk. She had no idea what this was about, so she couldn't risk assuming it was unrelated to what she'd seen last night on the web.

Jude's arm came out to stop her midstride. "It's a creek. We have to find a way around it."

"Why?" she asked, shouldering her backpack to a different angle. "It's barely ten feet wide. Can't we cross it?"

"Your foot," he answered, motioning at her right leg.

"Is waterproof."

"The shell is open," he countered, and she shrugged.

"It's not a big deal. The water will run out eventually, and then I'll dry it out. I'd rather cross here than go ten miles out of the way to avoid it."

"If you're sure," he said, raising a brow while he waited for her confirmation.

When she nodded, he knelt and untied her left shoe.

"Take that one off. You don't want wet shoes and socks for hours until we can dry them out. Does the right one need to come off?"

"Yes, or I'll be off balance," she explained as she sat down, quickly removing her shoes while he did the same. "I'm taking the prosthesis off. I could get in real trouble if the liner gets wet since it takes so long to dry."

"How will you walk?" he asked, hooking her shoes together for her.

"When they perform a Syme amputation, they retain the heel pad and wrap it around the end of the bones. You can walk on it like you would your foot. It's a bit harder to balance since one leg is shorter, but it can be done. I'll need to hold on to your arm to steady myself since I don't have a cane or crutch."

When she stood and took her first lilting step, he grabbed her elbow and helped her step off the grass and into the gentle creek. The bottom was rocky, so he was patient as she picked her way across to avoid stepping on the jagged rocks. When they reached the other side, he grasped her waist and lifted her onto the grass. Her body tingled from the contact despite the crunch they were in, which told her she might be in trouble when it came to this man. She pulled out shammy towels to distract herself and flipped one to him.

"You carry towels in your bag?"

"I do. They're great for cleaning computer equipment but also come in handy if I sweat in my liner. It's small but will dry your feet so your shoes don't get wet."

"I won't turn that down," he said as he wiped the sand from his feet before he put on his socks. Once they had their socks and shoes on, he tucked the towels into her pack and helped her stand.

"Don't they say that following a river or creek downstream will bring you to a town?" she asked. "Maybe we should follow it."

"It would," he agreed, helping her with her pack. "But that town wouldn't be one we could blend into. I know where we are and where we're going. I'm headed for a bigger city. One where no one will bat an eye at two bedraggled people checking into a hotel. We're almost to an ATV trail that will be easier to walk on, and that will take us to Deer Forest, where we can find food and a place to dial into Secure Watch."

"How long have you been working for Secure Watch?" she asked as they finally broke out of the trees and onto the promised ATV trail. At least it would protect what was left of her stamina after a long night and longer walk through the forest.

At first glance, she thought Jude was thinking about the question, but at second glance, she realized he was keeping a close eye on the edges of the trail. That was probably something she should be doing, too. Just because she didn't think she had more trackers on her didn't mean she was correct.

"Hannah Grace is two, so I guess I've been working there for almost two years."

"Who's Hannah Grace? It's a beautiful name." She sidestepped a rock at the last second before it tripped her up.

"Mina and Roman's little girl. They named her after Cal's longtime girlfriend. Hannah was killed in combat years ago, but she was also the reason Cal started Secure

One when he returned from the war. Roman knew Hannah well since they were on the same team in the service."

"A little tip of the hat to someone they both loved?"

"As well as a solid reminder that none of us know the impact we will have on the world until we're gone."

She knew the truth of that statement. Her entire life had been based on impacting others, even if no one knew she was Sickle.

"Hannah was born shortly after they put some of my former employers in prison, which was two years ago now."

"Military?" she asked, glancing at him in surprise.

"Yep, a major general in the army. He'd been stealing and reselling artifacts and treasures from war-torn countries."

"Wow. Classy and supersmart."

His laughter in response to her comment was loud, and she jumped, which told her she was more affected by the last few hours than she'd let herself believe.

"He may have gotten away with it if Delilah hadn't been able to find Lucas in time. Once they connected again, she could dig deep enough into her old files to pinpoint who had funneled the treasures out of the military pipeline. She thought she was preserving those countries' treasures for them when she was putting them into the hands of a man who planned to sell them for profit."

"Geez," Kenley said with a shake of her head. "I knew something happened when Delilah appeared on the radar again, but I didn't know what. I'm glad they managed to stop him, but something tells me it was at great risk to themselves."

"Not unlike our situation," he agreed, his palm resting

on the butt of his gun as though he did it all the time, but she noticed the tension in his fingers, which seemed to indicate he expected to pull it at any moment.

"Do you think we're at great risk?"

"I certainly don't think we're at low risk after what happened last night. I have no idea what's going on, but that much is clear."

They walked in silence for five minutes before she spoke. "I'll tell you everything, but I want to do it when we're somewhere safe. Distracting you now could be dangerous if someone is still tracking us."

"I agree," he said with a nod. "We're almost to Deer Forest, where we can grab a bite to eat and regroup."

"How far is Deer Forest from your house?"

"The way the crow flies? Less than five miles. Over twenty by car, though, to get around the forest. Someone would also have to know which way we went."

"If they find the tracker, they'll know."

"They won't find the tracker."

"We left it in those trees, Jude. Once they find it, they'll know we went one of two ways. We didn't go past them, and they didn't see us in their rearview, so they'll know we went right."

"When you took off running, I grabbed the tracker and dumped it in the storm drain where the street meets the woods. Trust me, if they follow the tracker, they'll be baffled."

Her snicker was loud on the trail. "I'll give you points for thinking on your feet." With a tip of her head, she sighed. "I'm still not going to assume we threw them off our tail."

"Whoever they are," he added with a frown.

"That's the hundred-thousand-dollar question," she agreed, pausing midstep when she heard a sound.

Before she could react, he grabbed her and pulled her into the trees. She knew the sound. It was an ATV rolling down the trail. She remembered the way the machine rumbled under her feet as it roared over the packed dirt, occasionally sliding a bit as it tried to gain purchase on the path worn smooth over the summer.

She tapped Gabriella on the shoulder. "Slow down!" The sound was lost to the wind, even yelling as loud as she could. Kenley motioned with her hands for her to back off the throttle, but Gabriella just laughed and pushed it forward, throwing Kenley back against the seat. She'd have gone sailing through the air if she hadn't grabbed the basket on the back. What was she doing? Gabriella had never been reckless while driving before. This felt reckless. Trail riding was meant to be fun, not terrifying.

Kenley leaned forward again, right into Gabriella's ear. "Slow down! Are you trying to kill—"

Then she was falling, Gabriella's scream filling her ears as she came down, something heavy and hot rolling over her leg right before she hit her head on the path, and everything went black.

"Kenley!" When she returned to the present, Jude was staring at her worriedly. "Into the trees, now."

He'd get no argument from her. They managed to lie flat on the forest floor and wait for the machine to pass them by. Jude had his gun out and pointed at the path, so she could only assume he thought whoever was coming was an adversary.

"Is your head in the game?" he asked without taking his eyes from the path.

"It is now," she answered to his nod just as the front of the ATV came into view. Relief flashed through her when the riders were not the men after them. An older man drove the ATV at the speed of a snail while a boy rode in front, pretending to steer. She couldn't hide the shudder that went through her, and as soon as they disappeared down the trail, she stood and paced the forest for a few minutes until he gently snagged her arm.

"Whatever happened on that ATV can't hurt you now," he whispered into her ear, sending a shiver down her spine. "Stay present with me so we can get ahead of the guys who want to hurt you." Then, as though he understood how difficult that would be, he wrapped his arms around her and held her. She exhaled at how good it felt to be close to another human. Her job was solitary, and she didn't date to avoid entanglements. She'd made that choice, even though it often left her lonely and unfulfilled. Her day job might be innocuous, but her night job wasn't, and she didn't want to get someone innocent wrapped up in it.

Kenley glanced at Jude from the corner of her eye and was sure he could handle himself, no matter the situation. For the first time in years, she relaxed into a hug and accepted the comfort he offered for a situation he didn't understand. That alone told her that Jude Mason might be her savior, but he was a risk to her heart she couldn't afford to take.

Chapter Six

Jude set the bags down on the small table in the hotel room with a sigh. The walk from Target to the hotel hadn't been long, but it had been awkward. He knew his computer and bag were safe, but he couldn't say the same about Kenley's, so he'd insisted she get a new bag and leave the old one in a dumpster behind the big-box store. If there was a tracker in it, their pursuers would know they were in Deer Forest, but that couldn't be helped right now. He had to touch base with Secure Watch and make a game plan before they took another step.

Kenley closed the door behind her and immediately locked it, then pulled the shades across the windows, plunging them into near darkness. Once he flipped the light on, he took in the room. It was a typical, skeevy motel room, but it was also the kind of place that forgot what you looked like the moment you checked in, and he wanted that more than he wanted modern conveniences.

"The first thing we do is call Secure Watch," he said, opening his bag and pulling out his computer and video screen. "The second thing we do is eat the food we picked up so we're ready to move at a moment's notice."

"Maybe we should eat while talking to Secure Watch," she suggested, bringing out the pastries, fruit, juice and hard-boiled eggs for protein. "That way, we can leave as soon as they give us an extraction point."

Jude knew that wouldn't happen but didn't want to tell Kenley. Secure Watch wouldn't pluck them from this situation until they had a better handle on who was looking for her, but he'd let Mina break that news should it come down to it.

"Great idea," he said, plugging everything in and connecting his hot spot to run through the lousy Wi-Fi the motel provided. He hoped it was strong enough to display the video and run his proxy scrambler. Once his computer was running, he dialed into the Secure Watch line and waited for someone to answer.

"Secure Watch, Whiskey."

Relief filled him. Hearing her voice and knowing they weren't alone made him feel better.

"Secure Watch, Jacko," he replied, using his code name to let Mina know it was him. Then he waited while the screen flickered to life.

Their greeting was a security measure in itself. If a team member didn't respond with their code name, the other person had an immediate indicator that there was a problem.

Mina's face filled the screen and while it was grainy, the connection seemed to be holding. "Jude, what's going on? That doesn't look like your living room."

"It sure isn't," he said, sitting down behind the screen and pulling a chair over for Kenley, who joined him with a pastry in one hand and a cup of coffee in the other. He'd never been more thankful that Target had a Starbucks inside it than he was this morning. "Mina, this is Kenley Bates. We've had an interesting night."

"Nice to meet you, Kenley, but I'm thinking maybe I don't want to hear about your interesting night?" she asked, her lips and nose scrunched up as she stared at them.

Kenley snorted, almost shooting coffee out her nose. "Trust me, it was nothing like that."

"We have a problem," he said, motioning to the woman beside him. "Kenley is a friend of Delilah's and called her phone last night. She needed help, so I responded."

"You didn't call it into Secure Watch before you met up? How come?" Mina asked, typing on a computer off-screen. She was probably running Kenley through every background checker she had.

"I didn't know what I had at the time until I talked to Kenley in person. She didn't want to discuss it over the phone."

"Smart," Mina agreed to Kenley's nod.

"Unfortunately, she was in Milwaukee, so it was a bit of a drive to do that." Mina's brows went up, but Jude ignored that and continued the story. "We were headed for her house when we picked up a tail."

Mina released a word fitting of the situation and Kenley grinned. "That's how I felt about it, too. It turns out I may have seen something I shouldn't have last night."

"It didn't start last night," Jude said, eyeing Kenley, surprised she hadn't picked up on it. Then again, she was exhausted, so that might explain it. "That tracker had been in your leg for at least a few days."

Kenley's eyes widened as the truth dawned on her. "You're so right! I should have thought of that." The sentence ended in a groan he could only describe as distressed, exhausted and frustrated.

Mina waved her hands. "Wait, wait. Tracker? In her leg? What?"

They took turns filling Mina in on the timeline of events until she momentarily leaned out of the camera shot. When she returned, she had a sheet of paper in her hand. "Kenley Bates, age thirty-one, occupation sole proprietor of Cyberlock Solutions Inc." Mina tipped her head back and forth as though she were impressed. "Right lower leg amputee, born and raised in Milwaukee," she read the paper as though it were a grocery list until she glanced up. "Impressive dossier."

Kenley was thirty-one, which made her eight years his junior. Jude should probably consider that way too many years between them, but he couldn't find it within him to care. Kenley carried herself in a way that said she was much more than a number. He couldn't agree more. Their lives might have just collided, but there was a familiarity between them when they shared a quiet space that had nothing to do with what they did for a living. It wasn't a sense of commonality in what they did, but more so *why* they did it.

"It's even more impressive that you got all of that in under four minutes," Kenley said with a tip of her fake hat.

Mina smiled a smile Jude had seen before. She was intrigued. "So, you run an upscale cybersecurity business by day, but you were hanging out in an internet café in a questionable neighborhood in downtown Milwaukee at nearly midnight on a Wednesday."

"That 'questionable' neighborhood," Kenley said, using quotation marks, "is where I grew up, so I respectfully dispute your use of the term. It's not a place for everyone, but for those of us who know it well, it's home."

Mina held up her hands at her chest. "Of course, my apologies. I was looking at it from the point of view of crime rate statistics that came up on my program."

"There's crime, I can't deny that, but good people there also do their best to survive. That's all I'm saying."

"And your family was once one of them. That's respect I can give," Mina said as Jude put his arm around Kenley. Her anxiety and fear poured into the room, flowing over him until he was compelled to do something, anything, to comfort her. "Were you meeting someone there?"

"No," Kenley answered, shooting him a side-eye and mouthing *sorry* before she finished her answer. "I was running my proxy scrambler through their Wi-Fi while my white hat turned, shall we say, a bit gray."

"You were on the dark web." Mina didn't make it a question. She didn't have to. A white-hat hacker would go gray only if they decided to do a little black-hat hacking somewhere. "Before we go any further, let it be said that we aren't judging you, right, Jude?"

"No judgment, we're just sharing information."

Kenley lowered the coffee cup to her leg with a sigh. "I'm known in the neighborhood as Sickle. When someone needs help proving a company or corporation is at fault for something, they come to me. Sometimes, I don't need the dark web to find the information I want. Sometimes, I do."

Jude suspected she was leaving out half the picture, but he'd let it go for now.

"But something happened last night that made you think you needed Delilah's help?" Mina asked to pull them back to the reason they had called her.

"It started with weird messages from a chat room. The sender wrote everything in binary code."

Mina rolled her eyes. "Such a childish game."

The snort that left Kenley's lips told him she felt the same. "Right, which is why I didn't give them much weight until I came across a program I wasn't meant to see."

"What kind of program?" Jude and Mina asked at the same time.

As Kenley explained the Spiderweb site to them, Jude watched Mina's eyes widen with each word. "There is another site I visit frequently, but I transposed two numbers this time without realizing it. That's how I got to the Spiderweb site. I wrote the new site down, but I don't want to type it out and risk it being intercepted. I also don't want you looking at it from Secure Watch."

"Why did you call Delilah then?" Mina asked, folding her arms over her chest as she leaned back in the chair.

"I wanted to go back in, but I needed someone to help me hide my footprints as I mapped the code."

"What about the program worried you?" Jude asked. "Besides the traffic cameras."

"Each new page not only brought more spiders onto the screen, but it also brought up new cameras even closer to my location. The last spider I clicked on showed me the camera for a warehouse two blocks behind The Matrix. We used to ride bikes past it all summer long."

"Are you saying the program could descramble your proxy and figure out where you were?"

"I don't know what I'm saying other than facts," she answered with a glance at him and then Mina. "I didn't know about the tracker at the time, so it's possible they were using that to freak me out and get me to back out of the program."

"Which worked," Jude agreed. "But that implies the person who put the tracker in your foot somehow knew you would find the program."

"That doesn't make sense," Kenley said, shaking her head. "Landing on the program was an accident."

"I'm going out on a limb here and guessing you've spent a fair amount of time on the dark web," Mina said to Kenley, who nodded. "Have you ever seen anything like this before?"

"Never," Kenley said with a slight shake to her voice at the end of the word.

"I would also guess you don't spook easily, so the fact that this particular program had you calling in outside help tells me you have a gut feeling about it. What is that feeling?"

Kenley glanced at him for a hot second before she turned back to Mina. He suspected he wouldn't like what she was about to say.

"Whatever this program is, it's not an innocent video game. At the very least, it's the misappropriation of public cameras for an unknown reason."

"And at worst?" Jude asked, bracing for the answer.

"At worst, it's a tracking system that could have grave consequences for the entire world."

Chapter Seven

Kenley swallowed back the bile that rose in her throat once she'd uttered those words. She hated even thinking it, much less saying it, but she had to be honest with the team. Keeping the truth from them didn't give them the chance to back away if they didn't want to get involved. She could go it alone, but she hoped she didn't have to, because if those guys found her again, she couldn't outrun them.

Mina was the first one to speak. "Can you get into the program and find its origins?"

"With enough time and someone who can throw them off my trail? Absolutely." That wasn't a lie. It was the reason she'd called Delilah last night. She had to get back into that program and figure out what it was, or she'd never sleep. Her conscience wouldn't let her.

"My thought was we'd come back to Secure Watch, but after being tailed so closely, I'm not so sure that's a good idea," Jude said as Mina shook her head.

"It's not. You know we've got your back, but in this situation, we have no choice but to keep you remote. Coming here could endanger the entire team."

"I was afraid you would say that," he replied.

"Kenley," Mina said, drawing her attention back to the

screen. "How long will you need to get back in and get a better feel for the site?"

"Getting back to the site won't be a problem, but it will take me several hours to better understand the code and who wrote it."

"As long as they didn't see your footprints from the first encounter," Jude interrupted.

"They didn't," Kenley said firmly. "I swept behind myself as I backed out, even though I never played with any of the code. All I did was click the spiders. Honestly, it's on the open dark web. I didn't need to get past a firewall or any security. Mistyping the fifty-two-character link to a different site took me straight there. That means they aren't trying to hide it."

"Which makes me suspect—" Mina said slowly.

"They want people to click those spiders," Kenley agreed.

"Why would they want that?" Jude asked.

"I don't know for sure," Kenley said, leaning in as though she was worried other people were listening. "But I think each time a spider is clicked, the program infiltrates the camera attached to the spider to get data sent back to the program."

"Like a virus?" Mina asked.

Kenley shrugged. "I don't know for sure, but that's my gut feeling. I'll know more once I get inside the code."

"But we still don't know why this program was created or why they want to infiltrate the cameras."

Kenley turned to him and made eye contact. "My gut says terrorists."

"Terrorists?" Mina asked.

Kenley turned back to the video screen. "Of one kind

or another. Either foreign or domestic. I'll know more once I get in there, but if they're getting data from cameras all over the world that are telling them traffic patterns, stoplight patterns, pedestrian traffic, and all those data points—"

"It could be utilized to plan the perfect attack," Mina finished, and Kenley shot her a finger gun.

"We need to get moving on this," Jude said, gripping his knees tightly. "Wait, could it be a Homeland Security program?"

"If it were," Mina said with a tip of her hand, "I don't think it would have a dark-net-specific domain suffix. It was dark-net-specific, right?"

"It was," Kenley said. "Which makes the government less likely to have written the program."

"But it's not a zero percent chance," Jude added. "There could be an underlying reason they're using the dark web."

Mina shuffled papers around, wrote something down and then held up the paper. Kenley committed the information to memory and noticed Jude doing the same. When Mina lowered the paper, she nodded at Jude. "You'll find everything you'll need there."

"Kenley, will you need anything for your limb? I have access to the basics like socks and skin protectant."

"A five-ply sock and liquid to dry powder if you have it," Kenley said, folding her hands in the prayer pose. "I brought regular powder with us from Jude's, but it's hard on the silicone in the liner."

With a nod, Mina wrote the items down. "I'll see what I can do. Once you're settled, I want updates as frequently as you can send them via video or text on the Secure

Watch phone. If this isn't a government program, we must alert them ASAP."

"Noted," Jude said as Kenley nodded.

"I'll do my best to get in there as fast as possible, but I also have to be careful so I don't leave a footprint or trail behind. We'll need to do it in phases."

"You'll have everything you need if you give us three hours."

"You're sure Cal is cool with this?" Jude asked.

Mina's gaze narrowed as she drilled him with an aggravated look. "I run Secure Watch, not Cal. So yes, I'm cool with this. When we're done here, I'll loop him in so he knows there may be government officials we'll have to deal with, but other than that, I make the calls."

Jude gave her a cheeky salute and a nod. "We'll take a break here and then move to the next station," he said, not mentioning the address that Mina had shown them. "I'll keep you in the loop once we're set up."

"I suggest you cover any tracks there before you head out," Mina said, her brow raised as though it were a question and not a statement.

"Ten-four," Jude said.

"Secure Watch, out." Mina waved, and the screen went blank.

They stared at each other for a heartbeat, inhaling a breath and letting it out before Kenley spoke. "How long will it take us to get there?" she asked, her eyes darting to the blank screen.

"It's an hour by foot. We need to clean up and fuel up, and then we'll head out."

"She said we'll have everything we need. What did she mean by that?"

"Car, clothes, credit cards, computers and maybe a gun." He took a bite of a doughnut, closing his eyes as he savored food for the first time in hours.

"But it's not a place to stay?" Kenley asked, sipping from her coffee cup again.

"That's unnecessary. There are plenty of hotels we can use once we're out of the area. We'll need to make a game plan for bouncing."

"Bouncing?" she asked, grabbing a hard-boiled egg and taking a bite. "What are we bouncing?"

"Our digital code, so to speak," he said, motioning at the computer. "We can't do this work and stay in one place. We'll need to—"

"Bounce," Kenley finished, and he winked as an answer. "We need public Wi-Fi to make this work. Internet cafés are usually the best and the safest."

"Not when you have Secure Watch covering your back," he said, sitting and wiping off his hands. "Our scrambler will be more than enough if we use Wi-Fi from a hotel. I tossed around libraries or coffee shops, but that makes us visible, and we want to be—"

"Ghosts."

His nod was tight and sharp. "Here's what I'm thinking. We stick to big chain hotels with good Wi-Fi. We move every second night and only at night. That way, we're never on anyone's radar, and we move often enough that no one can home in on us."

Kenley thought it over and held up her finger. "As long as we have a second exit."

"Always a first-floor room with a window or patio door," he agreed.

"Before you dig deeper into this, I want to give you an

out, Jude. You've been wonderful, as has Mina, but this may be a fight you don't want any skin in."

He shook his head slowly. "Too late for that, Kenley. The fact that I've spent any time with you at all makes me a target for whoever is after you. Whether that's tied to this situation, they know my address now."

"It is," she insisted, jumping in. "The tracker is confusing me, but I hope more investigation of the program will tell us why someone was watching me."

"Fair point. First, I would never leave you to go this alone when I know how dangerous it is. Second, until this is sorted, I can't return to my normal life either. They already know who I am and where I live. If these people think they can leverage me to get to you, they'll do it."

"Fair point," she said with a smile and a wink. "Partners?" With her hand stuck out, she waited for him to grab it, partly to feel like they were a team and in it together but mostly because she wanted to see if that slip of his skin against hers made her feel the same way it did the first time—charged, connected, protected and, oddly enough, owned.

Jude slid his hand inside hers and squeezed. Not in a handshake-of-partners way either. He squeezed her hand in a way that said he saw through her plan and wanted to feel the same things she did. Her gut reaction told her they weren't all that different after all.

JUDE STUCK HIS arm out to hold Kenley back as he scanned the property across the highway.

"A junkyard?" Kenley whispered from behind him. "Did she give us the wrong address?"

"Mina Jacobs? That would never happen."

"What are we waiting for, then? My dog is barking." He did his best not to smile, but he did, and she punched him lightly on the shoulder. "You can laugh when I'm the one poking fun at myself. That said, let's go."

"Not yet. To answer your question, I'm waiting for a dog."

"I don't see one."

"Doesn't mean there isn't one there."

"Bruh, are you afraid of itty-bitty puppy dogs?"

He turned a side-eye on her. "I've seen what a German shepherd can do to human flesh. If you haven't, then you should consider yourself lucky."

With her hands raised in the "don't shoot" position, she sighed. "Fair, but we can't stand here all day."

Jude took a moment to search around them, coming up with a rock. He pushed her back and lobbed it across the highway until it landed in the gravel entrance of the junkyard. After a sixty-second wait, he grabbed Kenley's hand and helped her over a fallen tree and onto the highway.

"I feel like your military training kicks in once in a while even doing this job," she said as they scurried across the road toward the junkyard. "That was smart. I don't see or hear a Fido anywhere."

"The army taught me a few things about looking before you leap."

"Duly noted," she whispered as she held on to his arm, staying halfway behind him as they walked. "But this place makes me nervous. Why would Mina send us here?"

"Where there's a junkyard, there's—"

"Cars," she finished, slapping herself on the forehead with her palm.

"That's my working theory, at least," he agreed as they

approached a tall white fence facing the road. Sliding doors at the center of the fence would open for a car to pass through. However, they were closed. "I don't know for sure, so stay close until we know we're in the right place."

"Any closer, and you'd be giving me a piggyback ride," she mumbled.

The comment made him laugh on the inside, but his concentration was focused on everything around them as they moved toward the white fence with caution. He had his Sig at his waist with his holster unsnapped just in case there was a sneak attack coming.

"I don't see a door," she whispered. "Are we supposed to announce ourselves? Dance? Clap our hand—"

She hadn't finished the word when the large sliding door parted just wide enough for them to enter.

"Camera," he whispered when she jumped in surprise. "They know we're here."

Jude grasped her hand, and they walked through the opening into what could only be described as a place where cars went to die. Every car make, model, brand and age was parked or stacked as far as the eye could see. He noticed an office to the right of them, and he pulled Kenley along by her hand, careful not to walk faster than she could. He feared she'd fall if he didn't take things at her pace. She'd kept up with him for the hike, but he could tell she was tired, sore, and needed a breather. Hopefully, he was about to give her one.

Then he spied it. Next to the office door was a lineup of stickers, including payments they accepted and didn't accept and car brands they sold parts for. Stuck in the middle of the other stickers was an image of two pistols crossed.

Jude tapped it before he opened the office door. "That's why we're here," he told her. "That's the army police insignia. Cal was Special Ops army police. I would guess we're about to meet another."

"It's all making sense now," she whispered as he held the door open for her to enter.

They walked in, both comfortable with the situation now that they knew the person behind the counter was there to help and not hurt. He snapped his holster over the pistol and waited for what felt like an eternity.

"Is there a bell or something to ring?" she finally asked. "Something about this doesn't feel right."

Jude was starting to feel the same way, but this was the address Mina had sent them to. "They have to know we're here. They opened the door for us."

"I know you're here, son," a voice said from the back of the shop.

Jude immediately went for his gun but paused when he saw the man walking toward them. He was eighty if he was a day, wore an eye patch over his left eye, and carried a cane.

"I'm no threat to ya, boy," he said, his laughter alluding to the years of smoking he'd done in his life. "Mina said you're ex-army. I can tell."

"Yes, sir," Jude said, shaking the man's hand when he arrived at the desk. "I was cyber intel."

"Good to meet you. I'm an old friend of Cal's—the name's Archie. I've owned this junkyard longer than you've been alive. I hoped my son would take it over one day, but I never had one, so I guess that's not going to happen."

Archie bent over laughing until he started coughing,

his lungs seemingly going to be the death of him. He stood up and dug around in his pocket. "You wouldn't know it by looking, but I have a few clunkers around here that still run." He pulled a key from his pocket and thrust it at Jude. "It will getcha where you need to go."

Jude accepted the key with a grateful smile. "Thanks, Archie. Much appreciated."

Archie motioned them to follow him behind the desk and out the back door of the small office fashioned out of an old metal shed. Parked in the back was a gray Honda Civic hatchback. It was probably the ugliest thing he'd ever seen, but it didn't have to look pretty to run.

"Thanks to our mutual friend, the plates are registered to someone who only exists on paper. Try not to drive it like you stole it, eh?" He started laughing again, slapping his knee. "But seriously, I wouldn't push this one past sixty-five if you want to stay alive."

"Noted," Jude said, trying to ignore the four tires that didn't match, the missing hubcaps, the downward turn of the bumper, and the piece of duct tape holding the back window up. It was more memorable than he would have preferred, but there was nothing he could do about it. Kenley couldn't continue walking, and they had no time to argue. This would never end if they didn't get back into that program. "Thanks for your help. I'll take good care of it."

"Son, I never want to see this ugly duckling again. Please don't return it. I don't need the kind of trouble that might follow you."

Jude understood his concerns and nodded once. "I'll make sure it finds a good home."

"The bottom of a lake wouldn't be a bad resting place,"

he said, motioning them around to the back, where he popped the hatch. "I have a few goodies for you. I followed Mina's list to a T."

Jude quickly took stock of the supplies. There were clothes, a second proxy scrambler, and nothing else. "Looks like we're set." He had to admit he was disappointed they wouldn't have a bit more firepower, but he'd have to make do with what he had.

"I hope it gets you to safety," Archie said, slamming the hatch. "Just in case you need an assist, that there blanket on the back seat isn't for keeping warm."

Archie lifted his brows at Jude, and he nodded, understanding. He'd come through with the firepower after all.

"Archie, you've been most helpful," Jude said, shaking his hand as he held the passenger door open for Kenley. "We'd better be on our way."

Kenley held up her finger and turned to Archie. "Do you have cameras here?"

"Yes, ma'am," Archie said, pointing them out for them. "Can't run a business like this without them. Don't worry, they're 'down for maintenance' right now." He threw some air quotes around in the air. Jude had to bite back a smile.

"I'm glad to hear that, but I have one more question," Kenley said. "Do you use a security company or take care of the recordings yourself?"

"A company takes care of all that for me. I'm an old dog, and those are not the tricks I can learn. Don't worry, they won't come back online until you're long down the road."

Kenley nodded, but Jude could tell that the answer Archie had given them wasn't the one she wanted to hear. "We appreciate that, Archie," she said, sitting in the passenger seat and pulling her legs in. "And we appreciate the help."

Jude shut the door once she was in, and the back-seat blanket caught his eye. He was grateful to Mina for getting them the long gun. He didn't want to shoot anyone, but he also didn't want to be in a firefight with only a handgun.

After a final handshake with Archie, Jude lowered himself into the car and slammed the door. "Here goes nothing," he said to Kenley and turned the key in the ignition.

Chapter Eight

They'd each taken a power nap before leaving the last motel room, but Jude could tell Kenley was still exhausted. They'd walked over an hour to Archie's and had been up for nearly twenty-four hours. He'd decided to stick to the back roads as they made their way into Wisconsin. The hatchback seemed to be in okay shape, but he didn't push the speedometer over sixty. He wanted to ensure the gun in the back seat didn't land on anyone's radar.

Returning to Wisconsin was a risk, but Jude was willing to take it to be closer to the team. If they got in a bind and needed assistance, the closer to Minnesota they were, the better. The plan was to find the biggest chain hotel in a city, check in and get to work. He didn't like the risks that came with a random hotel that he couldn't scout, but they had limited options at this point in the game.

"Kenley," he said, and she finally tore her gaze away from the window to look at him. "Why did you ask Archie about the cameras?" She'd been quiet for the last thirty miles, and while he understood why, he also didn't want her to draw so far into herself that she stopped trusting him to help her out of this situation. "I got the feeling you didn't like his answer."

The woman next to him shifted in her seat and pinned

those brown eyes on him. He had to keep his pointed at the road, or he would start thinking about how sweet she would feel under his hands and his lips. It wasn't a good idea to drive distracted, so he forced himself to concentrate on the problem they had to solve.

"Not his answer specifically," she explained. "More the idea of it. I've been thinking about the program and have many questions. If this Spiderweb website gets access to a camera, does it also get access to all the saved data, or can it only get the data from the moment it gets access to it on forward? Does that make sense?"

Jude tossed it around in his head for a moment. "Because it would somehow use the prior data to its advantage?"

"That's my working theory right now," she said. "I'm trying to look at it from all angles, but every time I do, another angle pops up." Kenley rubbed her forehead as though she was frustrated and tired. "Part of me wants this to be a dumb game created by some kid who thinks it's funny. My embarrassment about overreacting would be leaps and bounds less destructive than what a terrorist would do with the information."

"But you can't convince yourself it's a dumb game created by some kid?"

"The tracker in my shoe and the guys in the truck are hard to explain away, but I do a lot of digging on the dark web."

"If you think about it," Jude said, his thoughts following that path, "it has to be a coincidence."

"Because of the tracker," she said, and he nodded. "I thought of that, too. The tracker was in my shoe before I found the site, which means the Spiderweb program has nothing to do with it."

"It also means we're back at square one in figuring out who put the tracker in your shoe and why."

"My brain hurts," she moaned, tossing her head back on the headrest. "In my opinion, that's less important right now. What's important is figuring out what the Spiderweb program is and why it's there. It could spiral out of control quickly if we don't stop it. What do you think?"

"We're in full agreement. I hope whoever is behind the spiders has no idea anyone found it."

"Oh, they know," she said, holding up a finger. "They know because I was clicking the spiders. Even if all it does is send back data on what cameras came online, they'd know someone clicked them."

"Unless they're already all active," Jude finally said, giving voice to what he'd been thinking for the last few hours.

"Then why make the website?" Kenley asked in confusion.

They both fell silent again as they drove, the car rumbling under them as they made their way toward the Wisconsin border. The exhaust had a hole somewhere, but Jude was grateful for the wheels, no matter the condition.

"For a reason neither of us understand, someone put a tracker in my foot shell," Kenley said, as though she needed to talk it out. "Whether that has to do with my day or night job, I can't be sure."

"Or something else entirely?"

"I don't date, if that's what you're asking," she said, staring straight ahead out the windshield. "My parents are dead, and I have no living family in the area. There would be no other reason to track me."

"Okay, in that case, it has to be work-related and not personal."

"In the end, that's less important than shutting down this camera situation," she said, shifting to get more comfortable on the old seats. This car was probably older than she was, and time hadn't been kind to it. "If we don't, and it gains power underground and off the radar of any governing agency, then we're holding the smoking gun, too."

"We could just go to the authorities, you know," he said with a shrug. "You can turn it over to them to figure out."

"I thought of that for about five seconds last night before I laughed and said nah. Someone sophisticated enough to make that program would see a government hacker on the first keystroke. They might be cyber experts, but I haven't met one yet who is subtle."

"Hey," Jude said with a smile. "I think I take offense at that!"

"There's a reason I'm taking point when we go back in," she said with a wink. "But seriously, this kind of job will be tricky, and I suspect there will be plenty of traps just waiting to snare us. I'd rather do the recon on it myself to see who's behind it. One thing I know for sure is that it's not the government."

"We can't keep it from them forever, though," he said, slowing the car as he noticed the thermometer creeping up toward hot. Great. Just what they needed. He made a mental note to find a gas station where he could grab some coolant in case the radiator was the problem. For all he knew, the gauge was faulty, but he couldn't risk losing their ride due to negligence.

"I'm hoping Secure Watch will facilitate that information once we have hard evidence about who it is or what it's for."

"And if we find out it's a government program?"

"It's not," she said, shaking her head with determination. "You know how the government and the military work. This is not one of their programs. If anything, it's the exact opposite."

"Someone who wants to use the information against them?"

"Possibly. It could be cyberwarfare," she agreed. "It could be anything. That's why I feel like I'm sitting on my hands here. I need more information before deciding what we should do with it."

"To that end, have you decided where we're stopping first?"

"I was thinking Lake Geneva," she answered. "We can drive straight into it from either 47 or 12."

"Not a bad idea since it's enough of a tourist town that they aren't going to remember two new faces. That's only an hour from Milwaukee?" Jude noticed her nod from the corner of his eye. "Not ideal in terms of that pickup truck full of goons, but we have to hope ditching the tracker was enough to throw them off our trail." He pointed at the Secure Watch phone on the console. "Text Mina and have her get us a room at a chain hotel."

"We talked about that," she said, not reaching for the phone. "No calling ahead."

"We did, but then I remembered that since Covid, everyone has contactless check-in. We can check in directly from the phone, and no one will ever see our faces. We can check out the same way. Text Mina and tell her what our parameters are for a room so she knows. She'll have it taken care of long before we get there."

"You make a good point. The fewer people who remember us, the better." She grabbed the phone and punched in the passcode to open it.

He put his hand on hers for a moment. The warmth and softness of her skin seeped into his fingers and warmed him instantly. He hated to admit how much he yearned for the touch of another person. A solitary life was safe, but it wasn't comforting. "To start the conversation, type Secure Watch, Jacko. Then you wait for their reply."

She swiftly did as he said and then glanced at him. "You all have code names? Is that paranoia or purposeful?"

"Both," he answered, his gaze rocketing to all three mirrors to watch for a tail. "Cal, being ex-military, decided when he started Secure One that code names were a good way to protect his team's real identities."

"So, is the way you address each other in the opening sequence also code for something?"

"In a way. When we use that greeting, both sides know no one is being coerced by an outside entity that could put Secure Watch at risk. If you were to text without that greeting or with any other type of greeting, Mina would not respond, burn the phone, and send out the team to help. If I were to get communication from them without the formal greeting, I would ditch the phone and go radio silent."

"I get it now. If someone was in a hostage situation, you'd purposely not answer correctly so they knew you were in trouble. Smart."

Jude tipped his head in agreement while she tapped the phone on her palm. "Want to tell me the site that you visit a lot? The one you transposed the numbers on to find the Spiderweb page."

"If I said no, would I get away with it?"

He laughed loudly in response to her question. "Maybe for right now, but not forever."

"It's a site that holds the unpublished studies that a corporation does on its products. Studies they don't want as public consumption."

"They're using an I2P domain specific?"

"Yep," she agreed. "It's an invisible internet project domain-ending. By keeping it hidden this way, I can only assume they have a greater than ninety-nine percent chance that no one will read it. Without the exact fifty-two-character letter and number sequence, you wouldn't find it. That's about—" she paused and tipped her head back and forth a few times "—forty trillion different combinations of numbers and letters."

"But you found it."

"I did, but I was looking. I didn't accidentally come across it."

"The question I should have asked then was, why were you looking for it?"

"Evidence?" she asked, and Jude cut his gaze to her for a moment.

"The reaction you had on the trail this morning to the sound of the ATV. I've seen that before, always as a PTSD response. You went somewhere. Where did you go?"

The phone beeped, drawing Kenley's attention to the screen where she read the message. "She replied, Secure Watch, Whiskey, go ahead with your message."

"Good. Ask her to stick to hotels that have digital room

keys. We want to bypass as many reception desks as possible."

Kenley nodded and typed until the message was sent. "With any luck, we can be inside that site by dinnertime."

"We need food and sleep before we do anything," he said firmly. "After a hot meal and a good night's sleep, we'll commence the work."

"You're forgetting that most hotels have noon or before checkout times."

"We'll be paying for two full nights even though we'll check out at midnight. There's no other way. Then we'll drive a few hours, check into a new place, and repeat the process."

"We might not need to," she argued. "Those guys haven't turned up since we ditched the tracker. Staying put means we find the answers faster."

"You're not wrong," he agreed as they flew by a sign telling them Lake Geneva was exactly two hours away. "But we don't want to be on anyone's Wi-Fi network longer than a day before we move. Secure Watch has strong scramblers, but it's smarter to use a new host as often as possible, considering what we'll be doing."

"Okay," she agreed, turning to him. "But you have to be flexible with the timeline. If we're in the middle of something at midnight, we might have to push leaving back an hour while we finish. Agreed?"

"We can assess our leave times as necessary. Now, you didn't answer my question."

"You didn't ask one," she said, confused when he glanced at her.

"I did. I asked you where you went this morning on that ATV trail."

"Oh, that," she said with a sigh. "It was nothing. It was just an old memory."

"Didn't seem like a good one. You were shaking, and I worried you were going to vomit. You mentioned earlier that you killed your best friend when you became an amputee. Were you driving an ATV?"

Jude watched her cross her arms defiantly over her chest and stare straight ahead as though he didn't exist in the old Honda. Kenley had been a champ and kept up with him for the four-mile walk to pick up the car, but he could tell the lack of sleep was starting to catch up with her. He'd also noticed her shifting in the seat, turning her right leg one way and then the other every few minutes as though she was in pain.

"We still have a long drive ahead of us. If you need to take your prosthesis off to be more comfortable, that's okay."

"I don't think it's smart to be vulnerable, Jude."

She wasn't talking about her leg now. It was the way she said *vulnerable* that made his gut clench. He'd spent the last six years trying to protect the vulnerable. Her words sent a jolt of understanding through him. His entire life was built around this moment. The moment a job became something more. Someone more. That was a scary idea for a guy who had survived the last thirty-nine years alone on this planet for good reasons. Caring about someone made you vulnerable. That was something he couldn't afford to be.

Kenley stared out the window again, and he glanced at her side profile. She was so damn beautiful, but the most beautiful part of her was her brain. The way she cared about protecting others with her skills turned him on more than anything else about her. Watching her walk across that creek this morning on nothing but a tiny pad at the bottom of her leg showed him the strength and determination she had to finish what she started, no matter the cost.

Jude bit back the demand on his tongue. He wanted to know more about her, but she had to be willing to offer it. Demanding information was never the way to go about it, but if he were patient, she'd open up to him in her own time. If there was one thing the military had taught him, it was patience.

Chapter Nine

The car had gotten them across the border into Wisconsin before it started to overheat, and it required another hour to cool off enough for him to fix it. They'd taken advantage of the break, bought food from a small diner, and eaten it at a picnic table under a tree. Kenley had convinced Jude that it was safer than a booth in the diner. They needed to avoid as many cameras as possible, considering what they were up against. She'd even gone so far as to wear a mask into the diner to grab the food.

Thankfully, Mina had found a hotel with digital keys and got them a room with two beds. They could check in without making contact with anyone, and once they had, Jude insisted they clean up and take a nap before they started working. While she'd wanted to argue with him, her eyes betrayed her by drooping while he was showering, and that was the last thing she remembered until she woke a few minutes ago. The room was dark, and the clock read 9:00 p.m.

"You needed the sleep," Jude said from the other bed.

Surprised, she sat up. "I didn't know you were awake."

"I heard you stirring. How's your leg?" he asked, sitting up and stretching.

They'd found two backpacks in the old hatchback, and

the clothes he'd included for Jude were dry tech shirts that hugged every ridge of his well-defined chest. He might work with computers for a living, but if what lay under that shirt was any indication, he still visited the gym regularly.

Her bag held several changes of clothes, the powder and socks she requested, and a stocked first aid kit. She'd never been more grateful for the bottle of Tylenol than she had been when she shook two into her hand and swallowed them. Her leg was aching from the hours over rough terrain in a prosthesis made for city living. Jude was intuitive and, without being told her limitations, was able to help her navigate through the forest. He had saved her life. There was no question in her mind. If he hadn't answered the phone, she would already be in the hands of the people who wanted her—even if she didn't know why.

"How's your leg?" he asked again, scooting to the end of the bed to pull on his shoes. His jeans looked buttery soft and hugged his muscular thighs with every movement. Something told her Jude liked to run or bike when he wasn't lifting weights at the gym.

"No problems." She was going for sunny and unbothered, but the truth was something else. Her leg was sore, but that was to be expected. The Syme socket she was wearing wasn't the best for long-distance walking.

"You may as well know that I can already tell when you're lying to me," he said, strapping on his watch and sliding his glasses onto his face. "A little twitch at the corner of your right eye gives you away every time."

Instinctively, she raised her hand to caress the corner of her eye. "If you want the truth, it's sore but won't hold us up."

"I'm not worried about it holding us up," he said, sitting on the edge of the bed, holding her powder and liner. "I'm worried about you being in pain and ignoring a problem."

"It's sore from the uneven terrain, that's all," she assured him. "A Syme foot has low clearance because our limbs are long. That means we get very little dynamic return from the prosthetic foot. Amputees with shorter limbs have more clearance and can use sockets and feet that offer a better response to uneven ground."

"I didn't know that. Would it have been better for them to have amputated higher?"

"Absolutely, and I wish they had, but the situation called for a Syme, so that's what they did. I wish they'd gone below the knee, as that would have offered me better prosthetic options. It is what it is, but in these situations, I feel my disability more than I do in the city." She couldn't bring herself to look at him and see pity in his eyes, so she motioned at his hands instead. "Where did you find my liner?"

"You must have worked it off in your sleep. When I came out, I found it on the bed, so I asked Mina how to clean it so it was ready. She also explained how to inspect your limb for any blisters and how to treat them."

"You don't need to do that." Her immediate hand-waving indicated how uncomfortable the idea made her. "I checked it over last night. It's fine."

"Mina said you would say that, but she also pointed out you're likely to give it a quick glance and nothing more because you're used to it. I'm not, so I'll likely see something you might miss. I'll get your lotion on while I'm doing it."

"Can't say I'm super comfortable with that idea, kind sir," she said haughtily, glad the blanket covered her legs.

"Then it's time to get real comfortable, real fast, Kenley." He said those words in a no-questions-asked way. "We're a team, and if we're going to be a team, then I have to know your baseline. If I don't know your baseline, I can't watch for a developing problem. Our situation is precarious and an injury to your limb could put us in extreme danger."

"Are you using your military voodoo on me now or something?"

"No, I'm using my *common-sense voodoo* on you now. Is it working?"

A frustrated sigh escaped her lips as she pulled the blankets off. "You don't want to see this, Jude. It's gnarly."

"I'm thirty-nine years old, Kenley. This isn't my first rodeo." That was his only reply, aside from his fingers waving in the air for her to give him her leg.

"Probably not like this one," she muttered before she scooted up to the headboard. Did she want to show Jude her leg? No, not even a little bit, but he was correct that an injury to her limb would slow them down too much and maybe put their lives at risk. That said, showing a cute guy your amputated limb was vulnerable on a level that she hated. Without much choice, she sighed and pulled her pant leg up. There was her leg in all its glory—or rather, what was left of it. "I can't shave my leg, which makes inspecting the skin harder."

"Why is that?" he asked, inspecting the limb as though none of the scars that crisscrossed it, nor the matchstick thin bones nor the bulbous pad of displaced skin and muscle at the bottom bothered him in the least. Instead, he held her limb gently, glancing up to make eye contact with her before returning to the leg to check for skin break-down. She wasn't used to anyone else touching her leg, much less caressing it with such tenderness. How he held it and ran his fingers over the heel pad was a sensation she'd remember for the rest of her life. The look in his eyes said he wanted to heal her with his touch. There was something else there, too. A look of longing to connect? A desire to know someone deeper than he knew himself?

It took her a moment to remember the question and an-swer it. "Uh, um, it can block hair follicles, which leads to infection."

"I had no idea that was a thing," he admitted, rubbing his finger over a spot just below her knee. She shivered as his skin brushed against hers and raised goose bumps across her arms. "There's no hair here, though."

"My prosthesis rubs it off," she explained to his raised brow. "The socket designs for my type of amputation are limited. I hear there are some new ones out there, but I don't have coverage for prostheses, so I have to use what I can afford."

"You didn't get a settlement from the accident?"

"I lived in a questionable neighborhood, remember?" she asked, unable to stop the eye roll that followed.

"Mina didn't mean anything by that, Kenley." He cra-dled her leg in both hands, and his warmth seeped into her. Slowly, she relaxed her hip until the weight of her leg, and maybe some of the world, was in his hands. "She's not that kind of person."

Kenley leaned her head back against the pillow and sighed. "I know, and the neighborhood has changed since

I lived there, but growing up, I didn't know that. It was home, you know?"

He nodded as he lowered her leg to rest on a pillow. "I get that. We all have different childhood experiences, and they shape who we are as adults. From what I've seen, your childhood experiences taught you perseverance and a never-give-up attitude that still serves you well. Never apologize for that, okay?" He leaned on the bed and made eye contact until she nodded. It took her a moment because she found herself lost in his eyes. They were shining green this morning, but they told her how too many of his adult experiences had shaped who he was now. "You have a blister on the outside bottom of the leg."

"Really?"

He motioned for her to sit up, and she looked down at the heel pad. She was more than surprised to see he was right. "I didn't even see that."

"Probably because you didn't check, right?" he asked, grabbing the first aid kit Mina had sent along and walking back to the bed. "Tell me what to do."

"I can do it." She held her hand out for the kit, but he didn't move until she sighed and leaned back against the headboard again.

"Wipe it down, dry it, and cover it with the clear bandage you'll find in there. Make sure there aren't any wrinkles in the bandage, or that will cause more skin breakdown as I walk on it."

"When did the neighborhood change?" He followed her directions, and the swipe of the antiseptic wipe on her skin made her hiss. "Sorry." He offered her a wink, and she glanced away, embarrassed by the situation, even though he was more than cool with it.

"It was always a poor neighborhood, but it wasn't until the drugs moved in that it developed that reputation. I grew up in a small house with neighbors of mixed ethnicities. My mom was Latina, and my dad was ███████. I was their only child. My best friend, Gabriella, lived with her mom, who was a nurse. Her mom and dad were from Guatemala, but her dad died when she was just a baby. Her mom worked nights, so Gabriella slept at our house, and my mom got us ready for school."

"Which explains the best friends part." He waved a piece of paper over the wound to dry it as he prepared the bandage with the other hand.

"We were for a decade." Was she going to tell him what happened? Could she lay herself bare in a room where only the two of them existed? Did she have the strength to tell him how she got her best friend killed without crying? The answer was no. She never could, but she could see the determination in his eyes. He was going to keep hounding her about it until she told him.

"The summer before we started our freshmen year, Gabriella's mom bought her a used four-wheeler. There was a trail that ran behind our houses, so we'd go riding almost every day. It was the day before school started, and I begged her to take it out one last time. A final goodbye to summer." Kenley's voice broke, and she cleared her throat, forcing herself to concentrate on the way he smoothed the bandage over her leg and not on the memory of her best friend's final moments.

"What happened when she agreed?" he asked, as though he knew she needed help to tell him the rest of the story.

"Gabriella loved riding, but she didn't want to go. I

begged her until she finally agreed, so we took off down the trail, with her driving and me behind her. She kept pushing the machine faster and faster, cackling and jumping up and down like a maniac."

"She wasn't normally that way?"

"No. She was never reckless. I mean, we were barely old enough to drive one, so we always kept it below thirty on the trail."

"But not that day?"

"Nope." She sighed and shook her head. "All these years, I've wondered if she acted that way because she was mad that I'd begged her to go until she gave in. I kept leaning in and motioning for her to slow down. It was so loud, and there was so much dust flying around it was almost impossible to communicate. Instead, she hit the gas and threw me back into the seat so hard it took me a minute to reorient myself. The next thing I know, I'm flying through the air. I land hard on the trail, and the machine rolls over me before my world goes black."

His long fingers had wrapped around the bottom of her limb, cupping it gently and massaging it as he listened. "Did she miss a turn because of the speed?"

"The trail was straight, so that wasn't a problem. All we know is that a front wheel sheared off, and when it went off, so did we. Gabriella was crushed by the machine when it came down on her chest and head. I was the lucky one." Kenley motioned at her leg and then closed her eyes, willing the tears to stay away since she had too many hours left to spend with this man.

"I'm sorry, Kenley. You feel guilty for begging her to take the ATV out, right?"

"Wouldn't you?" The question was defensive, and she

sucked in a breath to dial it back. It wasn't his fault she'd made bad choices as a kid.

"Survivor's guilt is a real thing, sweet pea."

Sweet pea? That was new. Maybe he wasn't a babe kind of dude, but sweet pea?

Or maybe he's trying to comfort you, and you should stop obsessing over it.

She rolled her eyes at internal Kenley while she stared over his shoulder. Maybe he'd think she was engaged in the discussion even though it was the last place she wanted to be. "Especially when you're guilty of murder."

He squeezed her leg while he shook his head. "No. You aren't responsible for what happened to Gabriella. You may have asked her to take the ATV out, but she drove it recklessly. ATVs will flip on a dime, but losing a wheel is a catastrophic situation you couldn't predict. Not to mention, you were fourteen."

Kenley forced her face to remain expressionless. She still didn't have proof that the company knew the wheels sheared off at high speed, but once she did, they'd pay for her catastrophic situation and a whole lot more.

"Some say I was old enough to know better but young enough not to care."

"Do you think that's true?" he asked, smoothing the lotion over her limb, making sure all her skin was covered.

"What I think is, we need to get to work."

His hands paused on her limb, and he lifted a brow. Jude asked the question again, this time in a way that demanded an answer. "Do you think that's true?"

"The one thing I can say about the whole thing was I did care. There's never been a reckless bone in my body, Jude. Gabriella, not so much. She loved to push the limits on everything, but she was bigger than me—bolder, stronger, braver."

"Not true," he said, handing her the special liner to roll on over her limb. She did it without thinking but did notice that he watched her closely. He followed each step she took as though he would one day do it for her. She almost laughed aloud at the thought. As if a guy like Jude Mason would stick around once they were out of this pickle. He was eight years her senior, and while she didn't have a problem with the age gap, his life experience would surely lead him to a much older woman. "You were strong and brave enough to stand up and tell her she was being reckless. Now, you do a job that requires you to be bold, strong and brave. Don't underestimate yourself, Kenley. That would be a huge mistake on your part."

"Do you have a girlfriend, Jude?" She asked the question without thinking but didn't apologize for doing so. The answer was important to her for some reason.

"I'm single. Why?"

She shrugged nonchalantly as though her heart hadn't skipped a beat when he said he was single. Jude carried her prosthesis over and removed the plate so she could slip her limb into the socket.

"I was thinking if you had a girlfriend, she would be a lucky woman to have someone as supportive and caring as you. I hope the woman you end up with knows what a gem you are."

"I'm not all that, Kenley," he assured her. "I have ghosts I live with every day."

"Maybe, but don't we all? What I know is no man has ever cared for my limb the way you just did. Most won't even look at it, so touching it, patching it up and preparing it for the day is above and beyond."

"That's caring about a friend." He reached out to steady her as she stood and seated her limb into place in the socket before she pulled her pants down over it. "The last thing I want to happen is you get hurt over all this, Kenley. Despite the tracker and everything else, I believe you're an innocent player. I may not know why yet, but my gut tells me it has more to do with you being good and them being evil than anything else. What do you say we start figuring out who they are?"

He squeezed her hands before she could escape the close confines of the beds. His smile was easy and relaxed, yet it carried heat that caught her off guard. The man before her didn't see her as a burden. What he saw her as she didn't know, but she did know she could trust him with her life, and he wouldn't let her down.

"Remember, Kenley, you're not fighting this battle alone anymore. I've got you. Together, we can find them and stop them."

He stepped back to allow her to pass, and all she could think was she sure hoped so because if they couldn't, the world was in serious trouble.

ELECTRICITY FLOWED THROUGH Kenley's fingers as she prepared for battle. It had taken them far too long to return to this program, but Jude was correct—there had been little choice. The rest and food were necessary, or they'd be too tired to keep their wits about them and avoid detection. She checked the clock on her computer. It was 11:00 p.m. If they worked all night, they might get a good handle on what this program was for and who was behind it. A niggling sense of doom reminded her that the person behind it was skilled, and it may take everything she had just to stay ahead of detection.

"Are you ready?" she asked, watching Jude prepare himself on the other side of the room. He would click the spiders while she ran the code. She hoped the code would tell her what was happening each time a spider was clicked. Once they knew that, she'd better understand why the website existed. She could leave it alone without a guilty conscience if it were an innocent game. But if it were something more, as she suspected, she'd hopefully be able to corrupt the code long enough to report it to authorities. "Before we start, I want you to know something." He glanced over and met her gaze with a nod. "Sometimes I wear a dark hat, but it's always for the good of the people. I'll make sure that's the case this time, too."

"I respect that, Kenley. It's also the only reason I'm here. I may not know why you turn dark sometimes, and while that needs to be discussed, I know that it has no purpose other than good. Now," he said, grabbing his notepad and a pen, "let's do this. I've decided to write down any identifying information I can see for every camera that comes online when I click it. You want me to pan the camera around like I'm playing with it, right?"

Her heart melted when he agreed that she was a good person, even though she didn't feel she deserved his confidence. She would accept his help and respect but put off telling him why she turned to the dark net for as long as possible. Sure, he knew about the accident and that she was on the dark web looking at research, but he didn't know the lengths she'd gone to over the years to convince big corporations to pay for their mistakes. Maybe she'd never have to tell him if they could sort out this site quickly. Something about the idea of losing Jude's respect didn't sit right with her.

"Yes, but don't stop specifically on a building or street sign to write it down. That would make it obvious."

"Right. I can use the arrow keys to work the camera while I write. Do you want me to call out the location for each one?"

"No, that would be too distracting—unless something is concerning. With any luck, the coding will tell me its location as soon as the camera comes online. I don't want to be distracted if that's the case. We want this to be a random game of whack-a-spider, making the cameras that pop up equally random. If it doesn't show in the code, it will be up to you to get as much information from each camera as possible. I'll call out if I can see the camera in the code, so you know."

"Ready when you are, Sickle," he said with a wink, his hands poised on his keyboard.

They'd already typed the address into their anonymous web browser so they could go in together, making it harder for one person to tail them both and splitting the focus of anyone watching the site.

"The sense of doom I have is strong, so stay alert," she said and then nodded for him to hit enter.

The Secure Watch router that replaced the hotel's router was robust and would likely suck a large part of the hotel dry when it came to Wi-Fi, but there was nothing she could do about it. It was late enough in the evening that they had to hope everyone else was bedded down for the night. It was hard to wrap her mind around the idea that people were going to bed tonight, utterly unaware that a program like Spiderweb existed. They went about their daily lives thinking they were safe, but the truth was the opposite. Safety was an illusion created by the idea that we control our own destiny. Nothing could be further from the truth.

She'd learned that lesson the hard way at fourteen. The accident had taught her that control of her life was not hers but fate's. The forces around you reacted to your decisions to determine the outcome of any given action. Then there were the things far outside your control, like the decisions other humans made in their lives that trickle down to yours. A prime example was the person who'd built this program. If their end goal was to wreak havoc and chaos in the world, it would trickle down into the lives of everyone in this hotel, town, state, country and world.

Before her eyes, the giant spider appeared, and she dug in, waiting for the code to load while Jude kept the spiders busy. If this was a kids' game, she expected the code to be easily read and changed, but that wasn't happening. With her fingers flying, she made attempt after attempt to pinpoint code specifics, but each time he clicked a spider, the program blocked her from mapping or changing the code.

"Are we getting anything?" Jude asked without taking his eyes off the screen. "We're fifteen minutes into this."

"Nothing," she answered between clenched teeth. "Whoever coded this is blocking me at every turn. I haven't figured out how yet."

"You're saying it's definitely not a video game for weirdos?"

She couldn't help it; she laughed. "Nope, I can say without a doubt it's not a video game. It's weird, but not a game. What are the cameras giving you?" Kenley continued to type, trying to beat her way through the code but hitting a brick wall every time. Whoever wrote this program was skilled.

"From what I can see, the spiders are set up in groups," he explained, concentrating on the screen. "If you jump around between spiders, you get random cameras. Some are US, and some are foreign, but if you stay within one spider pod, all the cameras on that pod are within one region or country. When you finish the cameras on one pod, another pod of smaller spiders pops out again, if that makes sense."

"It does," she said, pausing long enough to read the code scrolling across the screen. "What doesn't make sense is how they're hiding the camera information when it comes online." Kenley was frustrated with her lack of progress, but it was early yet, and she couldn't let the frustration consume her. She had to consider this a matter of life or death and couldn't risk missing something because her frustration took her out of the game for even a beat. With a deep breath in, she forced herself to stay calm and calculated.

"It's there," he said, his mouse still clicking. "You just haven't found it yet."

They fell silent then, both of them concentrating on their respective jobs. She'd broken through the first line of defense and could finally start mapping the code. "Some strings here resemble something you'd see in government coding."

"Are you saying we're messing in a government program right now?" he asked.

"No, I'm saying some of the coding resembles it. That doesn't mean it is. I'm going to send some of these strings of code to Mina. She can run it down for us while we keep working."

"What's your gut telling you?"

"That it's there to throw people off," she answered, still typing. "The rest is like nothing I've seen before regarding the government programs I've worked on."

Kenley quickly copied and pasted some of the code into a secure message and sent it to Mina with an explanation. Her suspicions were on high alert as she kept plowing through the code. If she was right, and she prayed she wasn't, she might know who wrote this program. If it was who she thought it was, then this game was going to be long, complicated and dangerous.

She heard Jude suck in a surprised breath.

"What's wrong?" Kenley asked, glancing up to see him frozen in place as he stared at his screen.

"I don't know how, but this thing found us," he said, his voice calm but his back straight. "I didn't realize it at first, but now I see that each spider pod has been moving closer to Lake Geneva. The one I just clicked is a parking lot camera across from Lake Geneva City Hall."

Kenley's fingers faltered on the keyboard. "That's impossible," she said. "How? We're blocked every which way from Sunday."

"I can only tell you what I'm seeing, Kenley. What I see says we get out now."

Their fingers started flying as they backed out of all their operations and cleared their computers.

"Get our bags together while I pack the equipment." Jude started unplugging the router and packing the equipment bag.

"We're leaving?"

"As fast as we can." He grabbed her machine and stuck it in the bag as she gathered everything else. "If they've pinpointed us to the city in the hour we've been on the site, I don't want to be here if that truck shows up again by morning."

"Fair point," she agreed. "But I can't figure out how the program is doing it!"

"That doesn't matter right now. What matters is that we know it can. We also know that with any other program, we would be phantoms, so this is a next-level situation."

"I would think it was my machine, but you were using yours to click the spiders," Kenley said, slinging her backpack on her shoulders and grabbing one of the equipment bags.

"While that's true, your machine was in the room. If it happens again, we're going to burn your machine."

"Absolutely not," she said, sticking her finger in his chest. "That machine is well over seven thousand dollars and holds my entire life."

"Isn't that a small price to pay if it means we're alive at the end of this?"

He stared her down, and after a few seconds, she backed away. Let him think what he wanted. She wasn't burning her machine. They left the room and headed for the parking lot, where the Honda sat like a giant metal blob. It was an '87, which meant the only thing older than it was Jude, and not by much. It smelled like cigarettes and bad decisions and was so ugly it was easy to remember. They needed to get out in the dark of night if they would escape unnoticed.

With the bags stashed in the back, she climbed into the

passenger seat, surprised when Jude handed her the long rifle Archie had hidden under the blanket.

"Just in case," he said as he slammed her door and ran around to his side of the car.

"Wait." She grasped his arm before he started the car. "You said the camera was in the parking lot across from City Hall?"

"Yes, why?"

"Do we know where City Hall is? We know that the camera is active, which means others could also be. How do we drive out of town and avoid the cameras?"

He tossed his hand into his hair as he let loose with a moaned cuss word. "I was concentrating on getting out and didn't even think about that. You're right. We know one camera is active, but there could be others. The only answer is you go incognito." He grabbed the blanket from the back seat and held it up.

Kenley sighed and nodded before she climbed out of the car again and got into the back seat, stretching out on the floor as best she could before he covered her with the blanket.

"As soon as we're safely out of town, you can rejoin the land of the living," he promised. Blob the Slob's engine sputtered to life, and it jostled her as he put it in Drive.

"I don't know what you've gotten us into, Kenley, but that website is no video game."

If nothing else, they'd established that before they had to cut and run, but the heavy pit that settled in Kenley's gut said she might have to negotiate with terrorists, and that could go real bad real quick.

Chapter Ten

The fuel pump clicked off, so Jude stuck the nozzle back into the pump and screwed on the gas cap. He glanced around the truck stop outside Madison, searching for any threat that might be waiting for them. His nerves were frayed after the last few days of running on nothing but adrenaline and fear. Not only had the program figured out where they were, but it had done it in such a short time that he was scared if they went into the program again, they'd never get ahead of it before whoever was after Kenley found them. She had fallen asleep within twenty minutes of climbing back into the passenger seat once they were out of Lake Geneva. While he could have used her as a lookout for a tail, he couldn't find the heart to wake her until he had to pull into the station for gas.

They were anonymous here just by the sheer number of people who came and went from a truck stop this large. They'd blended into the sea of faces while using the restrooms and stocking up on food and necessities. He had grabbed a couple of burner phones as well. Once activated, they could at least use them to locate hotels and use Google Maps. He was flying blind right now other than following road signs, which wasn't always the best way to escape a villain disguised as a computer programmer. At least, that was what Jude considered to be the situation. He also wanted some burner phones in case they had to ditch the Secure Watch phone and their equipment. Did he think that was going to happen? No. But two nights ago, he hadn't thought he would be in a car as old as this one, while on the run with a gray-hat hacker.

The driver's-side door creaked eerily when he pulled it open. It was nearing 3:00 a.m., and fatigue was starting to set in. He lowered himself with a groan and pulled the door shut.

"I should drive the next stretch so you can rest," Kenley said, unbuckling her seat belt.

Jude glanced at her and noted the look of trepidation in her eyes. "Before I tell you no, I want to say this has nothing to do with me being a man or ableist."

She lifted a brow at him slowly. "What's left?"

"Warrant officer of the US Army." She motioned at him to speak. "This is a four-speed manual transmission. While I don't doubt your ability to drive, I do doubt your ability to drive a manual in a car older than you are in the dark on the interstate with the prosthesis you're wearing."

"I could do it." She threw a little defense into her tone, but from what he could tell, there wasn't much pushback. "It wouldn't be easy, but I could."

"And if we picked up a tail?"

She held up her hands and then buckled her seat belt again. "You win, but I feel bad that you have to do all the driving when you're exhausted."

"They train that into us in the military," he said, pulling away from the pumps and back toward the interstate. "I can do it for a few days when necessary. Did Mina respond?" He'd left her in charge of updating the team and checking out of the hotel that they had run out on.

"No, but someone named Riker did?"

"Reece," he clarified as he flipped his signal light on to merge onto the mostly empty interstate at this time of the morning. "Reece Palmer. He's a core member of the team."

"Okay. He'll update Mina in the morning unless we have an absolute emergency and need the team immediately."

"Agreed. We don't know that anyone is tailing us, just that they can somehow see where we are when inside that program."

"I don't know how to shut that site down if we can't break the code," she pointed out. "I don't want Mina messing with it either, because if it does have tracking capabilities, it will lead whoever this is to Secure Watch."

"True. That said, we could still turn it over to the authorities. There's a real possibility it's their program, and we're messing with something that's a matter of national security."

"Oh, no, it's not them," she said, shaking her head. "I would have smashed their code in a matter of twenty minutes. The fact that I couldn't break through that code tells me whoever is behind this has intentions that don't align with the government's modus operandi. How long were we in the program before it started moving the cameras closer and closer to you?"

He pointed into the back seat. "I wrote time stamps on my notebook."

She unbuckled her belt and knelt on the seat, digging around in the bags. Jude forced himself to keep his eyes on the road, even though he wanted them all over her. She was the first woman in years who kept him constantly intrigued. Did she have a compelling backstory? Absolutely, and it was a heartbreaking one, but that wasn't it. Whatever this attraction was, it had something to do with the part of her she never let others see. Her internal struggles that she didn't tell anyone about were what made him want to be the one she shared them with.

He'd gotten a glimpse into her soul at the hotel as he held her leg in his hands. She hadn't wanted him to see her limb yet still she'd trusted him enough to show it to him. Knowing that nearly brought tears to his eyes. When she let him bandage the blister, he'd felt the change in the tide of her trust levels. She could have done the bandaging herself, but she'd allowed him to, all while baring her soul to him about how she'd lost her foot. His visceral reaction to seeing her leg told him he might be in trouble when it came to this woman. His protective side wanted to wrap her up in a blanket and lock her in a room where she could rest while he fought all her battles. That was a dangerous way to think about any woman, much less someone like Kenley. She was intelligent, driven, beautifully damaged, and far better at her job than he could ever hope to be. His insight into who she was had been appreciated, but he still didn't know why she did what she did on the dark web, and that was a mystery he wanted to unravel. It would have to wait for another day, though. Maybe a day when they weren't trying to outrun an invisible spiderweb.

"Found it," she said, flipping back around and buckling her belt. With his penlight pointed at the book, she paged through it and ran her finger down each note he'd made, finally tapping the last entry. "It looks like we'd been working about forty-six minutes when the first group of cameras turned toward the Midwest. We were in the program about fifty-five minutes when it landed on Lake Geneva."

"It only took them nine minutes to turn the regional cameras into city-specific ones."

"I bet it would have been another four or five minutes, and a camera would have popped up around the hotel."

They were both silent for several miles as they thought about the implications.

"Even if someone on their side of the program was changing the code every time you clicked a camera, there's no way they could pinpoint locations that fast. Especially when we've got our VPNs covered so tightly."

"No, you're right," he agreed, a bad feeling filling his gut. "But you know what could?"

"Artificial intelligence?" she asked, and he nodded.

"This feels like machine learning to me the deeper we get into it."

Kenley tapped out a rhythm on her lap for a moment and then grabbed their phone and started punching in a text. The phone buzzed back and forth a couple of times before she spoke. "I asked Reece to find us an internet café that's open right now. He sent me directions to Unchained Night Owl just outside Madison."

"I don't think messing with that program again so soon is a good idea, Kenley. Especially somewhere in public that we're not familiar with."

"We don't have a choice, Jude. We have to test our theory about the timeline. We have to stay long enough for it to put us in Madison. If it can't, then what happened earlier at the hotel was a coincidence and not a rule."

"And if it's a rule?"

"Then we run like hell."

UNCHAINED NIGHT OWL was like night and day when compared to Metro Matrix. Their clientele was urban college kids, which Kenley could glean just by reading the drinks menu on the small bar in the corner. There were also a few tables of college-age boys gaming together where, occasionally, one would yell out in victory, breaking the silence of the otherwise quiet night.

Kenley knew Jude thought this was a bad idea, but an internet café they could drive away from was better than a hotel where they had to sleep. She'd spend only enough time in the program to see if the cameras started moving in their direction immediately. They'd get out long before the cameras could zero in on them, or at least that was her plan. If they were dealing with AI, then every time she went into the program, it might make it easier for it to find her. While that would tell them that machine learning fueled the site, it would put their entire plan at risk. If only she could figure out how it was tracking them with such precision.

"Do you have anything?" Jude asked as he continued clicking spiders.

"No. Well, yes and no. I can read the code, but it's not letting me add anything to corrupt it. Every time I try, it immediately changes the original code."

"Which tells you what?"

"They're definitely using machine learning."

The sentence hung between them as they worked, keeping an eye on the stopwatch they'd set to ensure they didn't bypass that forty-six-minute rule. Her only goal was to see if the cameras could find them just by their presence in the program. She continued to try to corrupt the code while they waited, but that wasn't happening, so she turned her focus to the program's author. She had six minutes to figure it out, but there was no doubt it would take a lot longer than that.

"The author is using machine learning to hide themselves," she finally said, glancing up at Jude. "If the machine can change the code on the fly, then I'll never get ahead of it to break into it."

"Should we shut it down for this go-round?"

Kenley pointed at his laptop. "Did any of the cameras get close to us?"

"The last one," he said. "It was a restaurant camera about two hours east of here."

"That could still be random, though. Where was the one before that located?"

He checked his notebook before he answered. "Davenport, Iowa. That was a rather large shift if you ask me."

With her lip trapped between her teeth, she considered the leap. "Maybe, but were they the same pod?"

"Yes, want me to finish it?" Her nod had him clicking another smaller spider; this time, a traffic camera opened and revealed the intersection of State Street in Madison. That was only a few miles from them by way of the crow.

"Shut it all down," Kenley said immediately, backing her way out and shutting off her computer. "We need to get far away from here, grab some sleep, and then I want to bounce some things off Mina."

"Agreed. I think that was proof it knows where we

are," he said, jamming everything in his bag before they left the café and headed back toward the Honda. He'd had to park a few blocks away, which he wasn't happy about, but Kenley could see the benefit of not having the ugly blob parked directly in front of the café, which likely had cameras.

"Do you think it can do that without someone clicking the spiders?"

"I don't know," he admitted with a shrug. "But I don't want to be there to find out. Anything is possible in this situation, and all we can do is stay ahead of them by anticipating what they *might* do, not what they *will* do."

"It's funny how we walk around every day of our lives being tracked by cameras without a care in the world until we realize someone could turn them into weapons."

"I couldn't have said it better myself," Jude said, opening the car door for her. She noticed he did that every time, and she had to admit that she liked it. Not that she needed him to, but because he wanted to. That small, consistent gesture told her who Jude Mason was more than anything else. He was a protector, and as much as she hated to admit it, she needed one of those right now.

Chapter Eleven

The sky had that predawn look as they plowed through the night, but Jude wasn't feeling the new day vibe. He was exhausted. He needed to lie down for a bit if they were to keep one step ahead of this situation. Once they rested, he'd call Secure Watch. He hoped the team had some ideas on the best way to proceed. If he thought it would help, he'd turn it over to Homeland Security right now, but not while Kenley was involved. He had to protect her until she was clear of whoever was hunting her before he could even consider turning the project over to someone else.

Speaking of Kenley, she had been quiet since they left the café a few hours ago. Unsure of the right decision and unable to bounce anything off Mina, he'd decided to head west toward Iowa. It was the wrong direction for Secure Watch, but he didn't want to lead anyone to their door. He hoped Iowa had more cornfields than cameras.

"Geofencing!"

"What about it?" he asked, glancing over at her. The moonlight showed him the bags under her sweet eyes and the fatigue that tugged at her shoulders. She was strong, but he wasn't sure anyone was strong enough to shoulder a burden like Spiderweb. It was time for both of them to get a solid six hours of sleep before they did anything more. Doing a job like this while tired would only put them at risk of making a mistake and revealing themselves to the wrong person.

"That's how they're tracking me. It's the only answer."

Jude was silent momentarily before he tipped his head to the right. "Theoretically, it would work."

He knew geofencing was a technique used by marketers to track devices within a defined area. If a tagged device moved into that area, the marketer might text about a business near the person's location. The technique snowballed in terms of applications, and it was now used by many others, including law enforcement. If the police were looking for a suspect or a victim, they delineated points on Google Maps and then searched within that area for the device connected to that suspect or victim. Jude had seen the police use it for good, but there were those out there willing to exploit the technology and use it for evil. Many people didn't understand how easy it was to be tracked when you had a homing signal in your back pocket. It made sense that if someone could build out a program like Spiderweb, they could certainly set up a geofence for Kenley's phone.

"It's the only answer. There's no other way they could know where I was after we ditched the tracker."

"Geofencing works, but it's not as precise as a tracker, Kenley. They have to pick an area to fence, so there's no way they could drill down that fast on the cameras."

"But think about it, Jude," she said, turning to lean against the door. "Once they knew I'd lost the tracker, all they had to do was geofence the entire state of Wisconsin. Hell, they could geofence the entire Midwest. Once my device appeared on the fence, they could easily assign the AI to home in on me."

"If that's what they did, Kenley, we're screwed. It's going to be impossible to hide."

"Not impossible, just inconvenient."

"Unless they're tracking you from inside the computer," he suggested, cutting his gaze to her for a moment. Her brows went up, and she motioned for him to continue. "We know that with the advancement of AI, hackers can send a virus via an email that you don't even have to click. Just the act of it arriving in your inbox allows it to infiltrate your computer."

"Agreed, which is why my machine has no email service installed," she said with a wink. "My emails come in on a different computer."

"You weren't kidding when you said there was no way for anyone to track you."

"At least not through my machine, or so I thought. Geofencing wasn't on my radar because I didn't know anyone who would want to track me. Now that I know someone is, that's the only answer."

"Is there a way to prove it?"

She held up her finger and grabbed the Secure Watch phone, which would not come up on any geofence since it hadn't been tagged by the person setting up the fence. "How far are we from Prairie du Chien?"

"The last sign I saw said twenty miles, but that was easily ten miles ago. Why?"

"I would bet there's a post office there. We're going to mail my phone and computer. Then, as it moves through the mail system, it will keep showing up on the geofence. Essentially, it will send them on a wild-goose chase."

"We don't have to do that." Jude glanced at her. "If we stop and remove the devices' batteries, they won't show on the geofence." She must be tired to have forgotten that simple hack.

"You're correct, but if we mail them, it will draw them away from the direction we're going. That buys us time to figure out who's behind this program."

"We'll be down to one computer, though. That's going to make it difficult."

He noticed her shrug from the corner of his eye. "We'd be down one anyway. If we put the battery back in and fire it up, they'll get an immediate alert. That machine is dead to us other than as a distraction for our little friends."

"I must be tired not to have thought of that," he mumbled, rubbing his forehead.

Her laughter sent a shiver down his spine. A shiver of anticipation more than anything. He wanted to hear that laugh for years to come, so he'd better get his head in the game.

"Do you have a way to make purchases in this situation? I can't use any of my cards right now."

"I do. Are you thinking what I'm thinking?"

"Probably," she said with a lip tilt. "When we finish mailing the machines, we go buy a laptop. It doesn't have to be fancy as long as it has enough power to run the VPNs and scrambler. That's all I need to dig in and finally root out Spiderweb's creator."

"There has to be a big box store in the next town." He stopped speaking and stared straight ahead, his thumbs tapping on the steering wheel as he ran the last few days' events through his head. Who was tracking her to start with, and why?

"Tell me what you're thinking," she said, resting her hand on his arm. The warmth it offered dragged his tired mind back to the present.

"I keep returning to who was tracking you in the first place. What do you know that is so damning that they need to trace your whereabouts at all times? It can't be the creator of Spiderweb since they didn't know you would happen upon it."

He noticed her grimace, and it set in stone his determination to get to the bottom of Kenley's antics on the dark web. First, they'd get some sleep. Then he'd grill her for the answers he needed to keep her safe and bring this to a close.

"I will set that aside for now because it's a waste of energy, like a hamster running on a wheel," Jude said after a few moments of silence. At this point, he had no choice but to work with her if he wanted answers. "I like the idea of not being tailed, but when we stop at the post office, we'll mail my machine too. It's been in the same room as yours, so it's possible they were able to geotag it as well. It's better to mail them both and pick up two new computers than keep using an already tagged machine. Technically, the Secure Watch phone is dead to us now as well. That was also in the room."

"Hadn't thought of that, but you're right," she said. "It's better to be safe than sorry."

"I want to have them off our persons before we cross the state line into Iowa. That way, they have no idea what direction we went from the last place they could track us."

"The question is, what direction will they think we went?"

"My gut says if they know who I work for, they'll fig-ure we went up through Iowa into Minnesota."

"I have to agree with you. And let's not fool ourselves. They know everything about you by now."

With a nod, he tipped his head in assent. "All right, that's the plan then. We'll mail the equipment and head to Iowa. Who are you going to mail them to? You can't send them home, or they'll know it's a trick sooner rather than later. I don't want you to send them to Secure Watch. That's going to lead them to their door."

"I'm sending them to my business post office box. We know this will only buy us forty-eight hours at best, no matter where I send them. They'll catch on and know they were duped, but it will tie their hands just long enough for us to find safety and hack into that program without them knowing it's me. With any luck, by the time they re-alize I'm not with the machines, we've got their number."

A smile lifted Jude's lips for the first time in too many hours. "You think like a hacker. I can't say that I love it, but in this case, I love it."

"I am a hacker, and for the most part, my hat is white. I might dabble in the underbelly of the internet, but it's for a good reason."

Jude wanted to ask her what that reason was, but the lights of Prairie du Chien were on the horizon. He sus-pected the answer to his question would take longer than they had at present. "I'll pull over long enough for you to grab the equipment bag. We'll get the batteries out of the devices for now. That will allow us to move around the city untethered for a bit. Hide that gun, too. I'd rather we weren't arrested. Once we're ready to ship the devices, we'll return the battery to the phone so they can follow its journey. Where is your post office box?"

"Eau Claire, Wisconsin."

"Really? Why isn't it in Milwaukee? How do you deal with mail?"

"It's a virtual business address box," she explained as he found a side road to turn off the highway. "I didn't want to use my home address or any of the addresses around Milwaukee. It has to be a Wisconsin address, but the state of Wisconsin does not require it to be near my home address. I get very little mail at it, but it will accept packages. They'll hold the machines until this nightmare ends, and then I can forward them anywhere. Secure Watch won't be happy about you sending their equipment through the mail, but it can't be helped."

"It's the only way." His shrug said he wasn't bothered by the idea. "They all have to go together, or the ruse won't work. There's very little on that laptop, so it's not a huge worry."

After he slowed the car enough, he pulled it over onto the shoulder of an old country road. "Eau Claire isn't far from here, but it is the direction we want them to think we're going, so let's do it."

With a nod, Kenley hopped out and hid the gun in the back seat on the floor under the blanket. Then she grabbed the devices from the hatchback and slammed it shut. Jude had a handle on a plan that would allow them to eat, shower and sleep, then drive to their next destination before they messed with Spiderweb again. He wasn't sure if Kenley was tired or in denial, but she had to know the creator would know it was them the second they went back into that program. He'd use the next twenty-four hours to set up a safe zone—both to do the work and to find out what Kenley was hiding. Whatever it was might be more critical to solving this case than she thought.

Kenley climbed back in and handed him his machine. He'd no sooner flipped it over to remove the battery when Kenley sighed. "My brain isn't firing on all cylinders."

"Why?" he asked, glancing at her.

"The battery doesn't come out of this phone." She held it up as the logo appeared on the screen.

"That's why Secure Watch uses only older technology," he explained, holding up his phone. "The batteries come out easily. Also, if we have to ditch one, it doesn't kill the bottom line."

"Now what?" she asked, waving the phone at the laptop. "The battery comes out of my computer, but it's internal and requires tools."

"Which I have," he said with a nod at his computer. "But, if we can't take the batteries out of one, there's no sense in taking them out of any. When we get to town, we'll park the car at a restaurant nowhere near the store or the post office and go on foot to get what we need. As long as the devices are stationary, our cover is maintained. They'll know the last place we stopped, but they'll think we stopped for breakfast and nothing else."

"Fair enough," she said, turning the phone over again. This time, her brows went up. "I have a message."

"From?" He leaned over to see the screen after she put in her passcode. "It's in binary code?" Jude noticed her hand trembling as she held the phone.

"The messages on the forum the other night were all in binary code," she whispered. "How did they find me?"

"First, decode the message. Maybe it's someone else."

She nodded and set about copying the message to transfer into a decoder. Was this message from someone else? Absolutely not, but Jude would do anything to wipe away the fear she wore, even if it only lasted a moment. Kenley had him coming and going, which wasn't good. He'd made it a point to never get close to anyone. He had a job to do. He had a singular goal to save as many people from harm as he could before his days on earth were done. He'd participated in enough heinous situations in the service to know he had amends to make to humanity. He couldn't let the beautiful, sexy, intelligent, brave woman beside him keep him from accomplishing his goal.

Maybe she could be the one to heal that broken part inside that keeps you from living. Did you think of that?

He shook his head at that voice. It was dangerous to think, much less believe, that Kenley could be part of his life after this was over. You didn't always get what you wanted, and in this case, Kenley Bates would be the one who got away.

Chapter Twelve

Kenley took a deep breath as she waited for the binary to decode. Jude had put his arm around her shoulder, which, if she were honest with herself, made her feel safe in a way she hadn't since this whole thing started. Whatever showed up on the screen couldn't hurt her as long as she trusted in her skills and those of the man next to her.

When it decoded, she read it aloud. "Are we having fun yet? I know I am, Sickle. I do enjoy imagining your reaction when you found the tracker. Shame. Shame. You should pay better attention when you're in line at Starbucks. No matter, technology has been my friend since I was old enough to hold a phone. You may have bested me for a moment, but I will best you for all time when I shut down your side business once and for all. Ta-ta for now, bestie. 54V4N7." She dropped the phone to her leg and let out a long breath.

"Do you know 54V4N7?"

"That's his hacker handle. It means savant, and he is if I've ever met one. Not that I've met him in person, but we've tangled online plenty of times."

"You've been on his radar before?"

"Since the first time we crossed paths. I haven't been off it since."

"And now he's stalking you," Jude said, his words clipped. "He put the tracker in your shoe. Do you remember being in line at Starbucks?"

"Only nearly every morning, Jude. You said the batteries on those trackers only last a few days?"

"A week tops," he agreed with a nod.

"I was in Milwaukee for the last month, but if he put it in there, he had to know who I was. I never reveal myself online, Jude. Especially not on the dark web."

"When did that message come in?"

Kenley checked the time stamp before she answered. "Early this morning after we closed out of the Spiderweb site."

"Is it possible that Savant is the mastermind behind Spiderweb?"

"Anything is possible, Jude, and after digging into the code, I've had that fear in the back of my mind. I don't know why or what his motive would be other than to say he isn't afraid to work for people with a lot of money and zero morals. If a terrorist asked him to set up a site like Spiderweb, he'd say as long as your money is green."

"A gun for hire, just in a different way."

She tipped her head in agreement at the apt description of a man for whom she had no respect. Her reasons were the opposite of Savant's: she wanted to help people, and he wanted to hurt them. That made for a battle of wills that would never be won.

"We need to get out of here," he said, taking the phone from her and powering it down.

"You don't want me to respond to him?"

"Oh, no," he said with a shake of his head and a little

smile. "Let him sweat a bit. Do you know how to find him on the dark web?"

"We've run into each other online many, many times. He's never hard to find."

He shoved all the devices back into the bag at her feet, reached over, buckled her seat belt, and then turned the car around on the country road. "Then I say, we stick to our original plan. We mail the devices, pick up new ones, and find a place to stay. Once I've had a reasonable amount of sleep, you'll tell me what your side business is and why Savant wants to shut it down."

Headed back into town, Kenley focused on how she would tell him that story without incriminating herself to the man she was starting to care about a little too much. However, she wasn't worried about being arrested for her work on the dark web. She was worried that the man sitting next to her would abandon her once he knew the lengths she'd go to in order to get justice for others. The saddest part was that she wouldn't blame him if he did.

KENLEY LISTENED TO Jude talk up the Walmart associate as he checked out two computers, peripherals, and two more burner phones. He was smooth; she had to give him that. Jude was regaling the man with the story of how their apartment burned down, leaving them not only homeless but without any way to contact the outside world.

Tugging her hat down a bit more, she bit back a snort as she perused the book section next to the electronics, not wanting to be caught up close on the cameras. Knowing Savant had been near enough to get a tracker in her shoe told her he knew who she was without her having the same advantage. He was a ghost in more ways than one and not one that she wanted to confront face-to-face.

A woman with a shopping cart pulled up close, a little one in the front banging keys on the metal and making quite a racket, drowning out what Jude was saying. Kenley plucked a romance novel off the shelf, a guilty little pleasure she told no one about. She'd been reading the stories since she was nine, having found the first one on the table beside the couch at Gabriella's house. It had been about a private detective protecting a woman on the run from her husband's boss, who wanted her dead. She was hooked. She'd read every old suspense novel they had before she started on the new ones. Holding this one to her chest, she recalled all the years she spent with Gabby, giggling over their next book boyfriend and whispering late into the night, trying to decide who was the guilty party in the story. Kenley often wondered if these books were why she was the way she was. Using the dark web might not be the safest way to accomplish her goals, but it was effective.

"I just love those books," the woman said as she browsed the shelf, her toddler carrying on with the keys while singing a song to which only he knew the words. "I always keep one in my purse to read in the car during school pickup. It's the only time there's silence," she said, but she shot her little boy the sweetest smile. "The princes and sheikhs are my favorite. You look like a suspense girl."

With laughter on her lips, she held the book out. "Guilty as charged."

The toddler threw the keys on the floor as a finale, and the woman turned to pick them up, giving Kenley the perfect opportunity to escape. She met Jude at the edge of the electronics department, their new equipment nestled in the cart. She would have to find a way to pay Secure Watch back for all of this, though she had no idea where to start.

"Make a new friend?" he asked, slinging his arm around her as he pushed the cart one-handed.

"Just bonding over romance novels," she said, forgetting she was still holding it. "Shoot. Let me put this back."

He stopped pushing the cart long enough to pluck it from her hand. "Cowboys. Cute."

"Cowboy lawmen," she corrected, reaching for it. "It's a great series. I didn't realize the new one was out."

"You have been a bit distracted." Jude tossed the book into the cart as Kenley tried to grab it. "You deserve some me time."

"Jude." She hissed his name as he started walking again. "We're not buying that. I already owe Secure Watch wages for the next few years!"

"Then another few dollars won't break the bank, sweet pea. Next up, stationery and packing supplies."

"Excuse me?" she asked, grabbing the cart until it stopped between home and sporting goods. "This isn't romper room time at the store. There are cameras everywhere!"

"I know, and if you keep acting like you've got something to hide, they're gonna notice you," he stage-whispered. "Seriously, Kenley, no one watching those cameras is after you. Take a deep breath." He inhaled, expecting her to follow him, so she did, holding it until he let his out, too. "Now, let's pick up the few things we need to mail our precious cargo safely once the post office opens." He tucked a piece of hair behind her ear, still covered by the hat, and patted her cheek with a smile. "Relax. You'll be far less noticeable that way."

With her nod, he started off again toward the boxes and packing supplies. She hated to admit that he was probably correct about it all, but at the same time, this was nerve-racking. Chances were good that Savant was nowhere near Prairie du Chien, but stranger things had happened in her life. She wasn't willing to lower her guard the way Jude had.

She followed him, pretending to check out different items on the ends of each aisle as they made their way to the one they wanted. He looked relaxed with that swagger only accentuated by his backside wrapped in a tight pair of Levis. No matter how often she scolded them, her eyes wouldn't stop watching his every move. A little part of her prayed the boxes were on the bottom shelf, so he had to bend over to grab one. Her snort was audible, and he glanced back at her, wearing a smile that said he knew exactly what she was doing and fully supported it.

Once they'd gathered all the packing supplies they needed, he motioned her toward health and beauty aids. "What are we doing?"

"You'll see."

His wink told her she might not want to know, but she trailed after him as he weaved up and down a few aisles, stopping in front of the family planning section. He eyed the condom selection with a critical eye, scanning each package.

The awkwardness was killing her, and she had to say something. "Uh, this feels a bit forward of you, Mr. Mason."

He side-eyed her as a grin worked its way to his face. "It would be if I planned to use them for their primary purpose, but I don't."

Relief filled her for a moment before indignation set in. "Are you saying you're not looking for a fast fling with a one-legged woman while on the run? I can't decide if I should be hurt or angry!"

He turned and pulled her to him by her jacket until he could rest his forehead against hers. "I'm not looking for a fast fling. However, a slow, comfortable screw up against the wall with a one-legged woman cannot be ruled out."

"What's stopping you?" she asked, eyeing his lips. It would be so easy to press hers to his, but they were in the middle of the condom aisle at Walmart, so that maybe wasn't the best idea she'd ever had.

"Sheer will, and I'm hanging on by my fingertips, so don't push me, or I just might grab you on the way down."

His gaze drifted to her lips for a moment, and she waited, wondering if he'd take the chance of PDA in Walmart, but at the last moment, he stepped back, grabbed a pack of condoms from the shelf and tossed them into the cart.

"Every Secure Watch bag has a supply of condoms in it for uses other than the one you're thinking," he explained, walking up and down the aisles until he found the first aid supplies. "They're useful for all kinds of things, including protecting phones from moisture, which is the reason I'm buying them. We'll secure each phone inside one before we mail them. The rest I'll keep in the bag for emergencies."

It was the way that he said emergencies that sent a shiver down her spine. She knew she had to say something, but she wasn't trained in sexual innuendos while in Walmart. Before she could say anything, he did. "We need to get more of that covering I put on your blister last night. I noticed you're limping again."

"When we left Blob the Slob at that restaurant, I didn't know there would be a three-mile walk to the store. I may have to wait here while you mail the packages and then come back to pick me up." Kenley grabbed the right supplies and dumped them into the cart along with everything else. "Besides, there's no way we can carry all this."

"I've got us covered," he promised, pushing the cart toward the front of the store. "We need to check out, but we have to avoid the self-checkouts since they're covered in cameras. Then, I've got a ride coming to take us to the car."

"A ride?"

"It turns out, my friend back in electronics, Sam," he said, hooking his finger behind them as he searched for a checkout. "His mom drives a cab here in town. She'll be waiting for us when we finish to zip us back to the car for a little less than five bucks."

"What a deal," she said dryly as he started unloading the cart. Kenley moved in closer to his ear. "I don't think that's a good idea. We don't want anyone to know what we're driving, nor do we want to drag anyone else into this."

He cut his gaze to her for a beat before he finished unloading the cart. "If I thought we had a choice, I'd avoid it, but we don't." Then he turned to pay for the items, chatting with the older woman at the cash register.

Kenley felt terrible that they had to drag someone else into this game when she was the reason they had to play it at all. If she had kept her nose out of other people's business, she'd be at home taking care of her clients. Her heart skipped a beat at the thought. With the fear and anxiety over the last few days, she'd forgotten all about her business obligations. Would she even have a business left to go back to? Fear rocketed through her, and she bit back a moan. If Savant wanted to ruin her life, he may have found the way.

Chapter Thirteen

As far as seedy motels went, this was one of the better ones in Jude's experience. It was clean, quiet, and had a small kitchenette. He was glad he'd picked up some necessities at the store, and he'd promised Kenley when she finished in the shower that he'd have hot tea ready so they could call Mina for a chat.

She'd been unusually quiet since they left Prairie du Chien. They'd crossed the border into Iowa and stopped about an hour later at this motel. It was clean and seemed to be a biker hangout, which hopefully worked in their favor by hiding Blob the Slob. Kenley had taken to calling the old Honda that, and he couldn't disagree. It was a blob, but it got them where they needed to go every time, so he couldn't complain about Archie's choice.

Jude poured hot water into two mugs and dropped an herbal tea bag into each. He was beyond tired, but adding caffeine to the mix wouldn't help in any way other than keep him from sleeping once he did lie down, which he planned to do as soon as they talked to Secure Watch. The message from Savant ran through his mind, and he groaned. He wished he hadn't had to mail her phone this morning. Part of him wanted to hang on to it, hoping Sa-

vant would send another message, but that would be a
mistake.

They'd talked it over, but Kenley assured him it was
the best and only move. She promised that she had all the
tools at her disposal to reach Savant once they were connected to the web again. He could tell she didn't want to,
though. Something about this faceless guy scared her, but
from what he'd read in that message last night, that fear
was well-placed.

The bathroom door opened, and Kenley walked out
carrying her prosthesis and gingerly putting weight on
her right leg. She was wearing the lounge clothes they'd
picked up that were fleece and warm, something Kenley
never seemed to be. She'd bucked him at every suggestion
he made this morning at the store, not wanting to spend
money she didn't have. He respected that to a degree, but
they were in a situation they couldn't have predicted, and
little spots of comfort were necessary when stressed. A
warm pair of pajamas, a cup of tea, a good book. Those
were the only things he could offer her right now. They
wouldn't help her mental stress, but if they made her a
smidgen more comfortable physically, then he would pay
for them all day long.

She accepted his help when he put his arm around
her waist and helped her to the desk to sit. "You look
warm and comfortable for the first time in days." He knelt
and took her tiny limb in his. "Except for this." He inspected the spot where the blister was, disheartened to
see it had popped and was raw despite the protective bandage. "Good thing we bought more supplies. We're going
to need them. Can we take this bandage off and let it get
some air while we're talking to Mina?"

Kenley nervously glanced at the window and back to him. "Do you think we're safe here? If we take the bandage off, I can't wear the prosthesis. That means moving quickly is out of the question."

"I believe we're safe here, Kenley." And he wasn't lying. Now that they'd shed the machines and weren't carrying an electronic trail anymore, he figured they had at least two days before they could land on Savant's radar again. As long as she stayed out of the chat rooms that he frequented, there was no way for him to tag their new machines. "We're no longer carrying an electronic chain that was holding us down. We'll call Mina, sleep and then get to work."

"I'm not as confident as you are, but there's no choice. We'll let it get air while we fill Mina in and then bandage it again before we sleep. If I had an ice pack, I'd ice it while sleeping." She laid the towel on the floor and lowered her limb.

"Would that help the pain?"

"Some, but mostly, it would bring the swelling down, so it didn't rub inside the prosthesis."

He held up his finger, walked to the freezer and grabbed the bucket. "I happened to see an ice machine in the lobby, so while you were showering, I ran down and got some since we bought pop." He tied the bag full of ice closed and carried it back over. "There's plenty more where this came from."

"Thanks, Jude. You are a lifesaver."

After removing the bandage, wiping it down and propping the limb on the bag of ice, Jude sat next to her and dialed into Secure Watch.

"Secure Watch, Whiskey." The screen stayed black

until Jude replied, and then Mina's face flickered onto the screen. "It's so good to see you guys," she said, leaning back in her chair. "We've been worried."

"Nothing to worry about, boss," Jude said with a wink.

"A large purchase request came through on the card this morning. I approved it, knowing there was a good reason."

Jude noticed Kenley grimace and rubbed her back with an encouraging smile. "Thanks, boss. We've made some discoveries, which is why we're calling. It's time to fill you in."

"Namely, how we were being tracked and by whom," Kenley added, taking over the conversation. "Or one of the whoms, at least."

"Did you break through the Spiderweb code?" Mina asked, but Kenley shook her head.

"Not yet. Every time I got close to corrupting the code, it changed."

"And while the program was doing that to her, it was tracking me," Jude said, rubbing Kenley's back to keep her calm.

"Tracking you how?" Mina asked, her head tipped in confusion.

He explained to her that the spiders were directing the cameras closer and closer to them. "She realized we might be in a geofence."

Kenley took over. "That's the reason for the large purchase this morning. We had to mail our machines and the Secure Watch phone to my post office box."

"Especially after she got another message in binary code on her phone this morning," Jude added.

"Smart idea. That will make them think you're moving around," Mina agreed. "That also explains the new computer purchase. The binary code player again? Still no identity on him?"

"Oh, I know who he is," Kenley said. "His dark web name is 54VAN7. Savant." Mina sucked in a breath, and that surprised Jude.

"You know of him?"

"I worked for the FBI. Of course, I know of him. How on earth are you tangled up with that rotten apple, Kenley?"

Jude listened while Kenley told his boss how she met Savant. "According to the message, he's the one who put the tracker in my shoe."

"Did the message say why?" Mina asked, and they both shook their heads.

"Nope, but that's nothing new with Savant," Kenley said with a shrug.

"What concerns me is that he or someone he employed was close enough to Kenley to drop a tracker in her shoe," Jude said between gritted teeth. "Someone like that is unpredictable, and even if we sort out the Spiderweb program, she will still be vulnerable to that maniac."

Mina held up her hand. "Let's take one thing at a time. Kenley, I hope you don't mind, but I patched into your business server so Reece could cover your current clients. We also contacted those you had set up for intake to let them know you had been in an accident but would contact them as soon as possible within the week. Everyone was more than sympathetic."

With her hand on her chest, Kenley let out a breath. "Thank you," she whispered, her shoulders falling forward. "It hit me in the middle of the store today that my business could fall apart because of this, which is probably what Savant wants. I spent the last three hours trying to figure out what to do but hadn't come up with anything. I owe you, big-time."

"It's no problem," Mina reassured her. "Delilah and Lucas will be back tomorrow, and she can cover your clients until you return, which I'm hoping won't be much longer."

Jude shrugged. "I can't make any promises, but I hope the new computers will allow us to stay in the program longer before they realize it's us."

"That's going to be a good trick," Kenley said.

"Okay, they'll know it's us but won't be able to track us."

"How do you plan to keep them from tracking these devices?"

"I've deleted all the apps, turned off the location-sharing settings, and we'll use a VPN that stays overseas. Whoever made the program will know we're in it, but they won't be able to track us since the computers won't be tagged by the geofence."

"Mina, would you put some feelers out to see if the Spiderweb program is something the government is working on?" Kenley asked, leaning forward. "Some of the coding was reminiscent of what I encountered when helping a government agency with some bricking. I'm not at liberty to say who, but I also don't have the channels you do to ask questions and get answers."

"After you sent me those code samples, I did some digging. I could hear no chatter about it in any of my usual haunts. I did a deeper breakdown of the lines of code you sent, and while it's close, I think the same thing you do. It's reminiscent but not the real thing."

"Thanks for your candidness and professional opinion. I didn't want to be an island in that belief, but I've done enough with the government to know their code. That's not it."

Jude held one hand out. "So, we know Savant put the tracker in her shoe for his own sick games." He held out the other hand. "We don't know who put the geofence out for her devices and why."

"If I were a betting woman, I'd say it was when she landed on the spider site," Mina said with a shrug. "I've seen dark web programs do this before. It's likely as soon as Kenley clicked on the first spider, her machine was tagged."

"It still doesn't make sense," Jude pondered. "She uses a VPN for everything she does at The Matrix. There's no way they could continue to track her computer once she signed off."

"We all know that's not true," Mina said. "We are never completely anonymous on the web. When dealing with guys like Savant regularly, you can bet you're always at risk of picking up a bug and not knowing until it's too late."

Kenley turned to him. "Think about it, Jude. We used your computer to click the spiders in the hotel room, and they found us in fifty-five minutes. The spiders are putting us on a geofence, but I'm starting to think it's a completely different kind than we're used to."

"Can you explain?" Mina asked.

"You think it's more of a geofence that only works

when you're in the program?" It dawned on him then what Kenley was thinking. She could be right.

"Yes!" Kenley agreed. "That's why the AI slowly starts to home in on you as you click the spiders. The spiders are there to keep you clicking while the AI works to break through your VPN to reveal your real location."

"It's the only answer," Mina agreed. "Without the AI, it wouldn't be possible, but anything is possible with that in the mix now."

"My biggest fear is that every time we do that, a large swath of cameras in one region comes online for the program." Kenley was silent for a second before she waved her hands. "Okay, so we don't click the spiders. It didn't help us last time other than to tell us how quickly the cameras could find us. They aren't showing up in the code when they activate, so there's no sense in continuing to click. I'll have to find a new way to bust through the code."

"Wiping and reinstalling the operating system will clear any geofence. Does that also work for tracking systems like what you're talking about?" Jude asked. "We couldn't do that with our other computers since they hold important information that we couldn't back up on the fly, but we can wipe these new ones ten times if necessary."

"Wiping and reinstalling your operating system will clear any tracking system on the computer. I think it's only tagging you while you're in the program, but you're better safe than sorry. Also, when you restart it, you know the machine is infected if the system bricks," Mina explained.

Bricking a computer could be done in several ways, but Jude was often surprised at how frequently and incorrectly people used the term "bricking" when it came to phones and computers. If a device wasn't working right, but you could install a new operating system, it wasn't bricked since it was recoverable. If you couldn't turn it on, or once you did, the system was so corrupted that you couldn't install any operating system, the device was considered a brick. An expensive paperweight. Sometimes, it was a user error—someone might power down or unplug a computer while installing a firmware update. However, more often than not, the cause was malware. When big corporations had their system bricked, it could usually be traced back to a malicious BMC firmware—baseboard management controller—uploaded remotely to their server. Once that happened, getting them back online could take days, weeks, or even months, which was catastrophic for hospitals and other public entities.

"I'm on it, boss," Jude agreed. "But first, we sleep."

"You sleep, I'll work." Kenley practically rubbed her hands together in glee until Jude shut her down.

"Back me up, Mina. She has a blister on her limb, and it's swollen. Ice and elevate, right?" he asked, his brow raised at the screen while he waited for his friend to agree with him.

"He's right, Kenley. You know how quickly a limb issue can get you into big trouble. I don't have a way to get you antibiotics either, so you need to let your body rest and heal."

"Every minute we aren't in that program, those cameras gather more information. We need to shut it down." Her insistence filled the room, but Jude wasn't having it. They both needed to sleep before fatigue caused them to do something they'd regret.

"We don't even know what it is yet," Jude pointed out.

"We know it's not a video game, but we don't know anything beyond that."

"We also have no idea how long that program has been there," Mina pointed out.

"I do," Kenley said, pushing herself back up in the chair. "I got the date from the code. I haven't thought much of it until now. The program went live on July 4th."

"Okay, it's been up for three months. Another three hours won't hurt anything," Mina insisted. "Sleep, eat, and then attack. In the meantime, I'll dig into the government connection. Do you have a number where I can contact you? You said you mailed the Secure Watch phone."

Jude grabbed one of the burner phones and held up the number for her to copy. When he lowered the number, he glanced between the screen and Kenley. "Do you think that date is significant?"

"July 4th?" Mina asked, her head cocked in confusion.

"Independence Day," Kenley said with a breath.

"Whose independence is the question," Jude said, glancing at Mina. "Thinking about it for a hot second, it feels pointed to me."

"I was so busy trying to stay ahead of the code that I didn't even think about the significance of the date, but I agree with Jude," Kenley said.

"I don't disagree," Mina nodded, making a note on the pad next to her. "It could be the government making a point, or it could be someone who wants to use this country's birthday to make a different kind of point. Give me a few hours. I'll get back to you."

"Thanks, Mina," Jude said as she waved, and the screen went black.

"I should have realized that clicking the spiders activated the geofence," Jude said, leaning back in the chair.

"Don't beat yourself up, Jude. We assumed we were being followed because the cameras kept finding us after we found the tracker in my shoe. I'm relieved to know that's not the case. They only know where we are when we're in the program. As soon as we leave it, the tracking stops. That's good news. It means we can stay here for a few days without anyone knowing where we are."

"Until you go back into the program. Then you'll be back on its radar."

"I'll do it in shifts," she explained. "A little at a time. No longer than thirty minutes in the program since we know it took forty-six minutes last time before they found us in Madison. At the thirty-minute mark, you reset one computer while I fire up the second one. Right now, we're both tired. Let's get some sleep and then make a plan when we're rested and sharp again."

They both turned toward the giant elephant in the room. A king bed. One. Singular. Unfortunately, some biker event was happening, and this was the last room for the night. The bed was big, but it would still pose a problem for Jude. He didn't have the willpower to share a bed with Kenley and not hold her all night. She needed comfort, which was one thing he knew for sure, but that didn't mean she wanted it, and he had to respect those boundaries.

"I'll take the floor," he said, holding his hand out to help her up. "I can sleep anywhere."

He walked her to the bed and pulled back the covers. Once she sat, he lifted her limb onto the bed and stuffed a pillow under her knee.

"This bed is big enough for the both of us, Jude." He handed her a mug of warm tea and then grabbed the first aid kit to fix the blister before they went to sleep.

"Here's the thing, sweet pea. If I'm in this bed, I can't promise that my arms won't end up wrapped around you by the night's end."

"That's a bad thing?" Her sharp intake of breath, when he swiped the antiseptic over the blister, told him they'd done some damage to it today. Grabbing his flashlight, he inspected it closely, looking for any signs of infection. It was raw and bleeding around the edges, but otherwise, it was okay.

"It's a bad thing if you're not looking for that. Respect and trust are important in this game we're playing. I don't want to break yours by doing something unwanted."

"If I say I want you to wrap your arms around me, would that help?"

"Only if you meant it." He added a wink and lip tilt to let her know he was teasing but also not teasing. "I'm going to put antibiotic ointment on a bandage and cover the blister so you can ice it during the night. Once you're up and need to put the prosthesis back on, we can clean it again and use the clear bandage."

"That would be fine. I'm sure after some time out of the prosthesis, it will start to heal quickly. And Jude?" she said, and he glanced up from where he was opening the bandage. "I meant it."

Chapter Fourteen

Kenley wondered what time it was, but she couldn't turn to look at the clock without disturbing Jude, whose chest was pressed tightly against her, with one arm thrown over her hip to hold her there. She'd woken up that way about twenty minutes ago but wasn't ready to give up the comfort his arms offered, so she stayed still. The deep darkness of the room told her it was well after five, and the sun had already set. Considering they didn't climb into bed until after noon, it could be even later.

Now that she was rested, she was ready to tackle this monster monkey on her back. She had no hope of stopping Spiderweb until she could figure out who was behind it. Her biggest fear was that whoever coded Spiderweb had turned it over completely to machine learning, which would allow it to spiral out of control once more people knew the website existed. If others were clicking spiders on the site, and each click trained the program to grab more cameras in each area, it was only a matter of time until the Spiderweb program controlled every camera on every corner in every city. There were too many terrorist organizations in the world that would jump into a bidding war to own the data and control of all the cameras in the world. They could use the information to cause carnage at yet unseen proportions or incite another world war. They couldn't allow that to happen, no matter the cost to her. Somehow, she'd protect Jude, even if that meant they eventually parted ways.

Jude was the kind of man she could see herself sharing her life with if that kind of life was in the cards for her. She wasn't sure it was, not when she brought situations like this down on her head by doing something she knew was inherently dangerous. It wasn't right to drag others in only to make them fight a battle that wasn't theirs to fight.

When is it going to stop being your war to fight?

"How'd you sleep?" Jude's voice was soft and sleepy as he tightened his arm around her waist. "I dreamt that I was holding a beautiful woman only to wake up and realize I was."

She slid her hand down his arm until hers was over his on her waist. "It was nice to be held by someone who cares, Jude. I don't have those kinds of relationships in my life."

"Ever?" He instinctively pulled her closer even though there was already no space between them.

"My life doesn't allow for solid connections, Jude."

"And that has something to do with the dark web and Savant, right?"

She rolled over to her back, hoping he'd drop his arm, but he didn't. He just rotated it around to lay it across her belly. "My work is my penance. I don't expect you to understand that, but I've lived this way for seventeen years."

"Your penance? Do you mean for the accident that killed Gabriella?"

"Yes. She died, but I lived. Now it's my job to prove the accident wasn't Gabby's fault."

"The accident wasn't your fault either, sweet pea. Has no one ever told you that?"

"Of course, they have. Part of it is my fault. I begged her to take it out that day! When she said no the first time, I should have walked away. She wasn't in the mood and proved that once we got on the trail. I don't know why she acted the way she did, but I know if we'd been on any other brand of ATV, she wouldn't be dead. With her gone, it's my responsibility to prove what I already know."

"Tell me what you already know, Kenley."

She bit her lip and shook her head. It had been seventeen years, and she still hadn't voiced what she'd been doing to hold Staun Bril accountable to another living being. That was her battle to fight, not his.

"Let me ask this a different way. It's been seventeen years. How are you going to find evidence?"

"That's what I do on the dark web, Jude. I talk to people and seek information proving what I already know."

"What do you already know, Kenley?" He whispered the question this time with his mouth near her ear, sending a shiver through her. It felt like understanding, anticipation and seduction, as it traveled from her head to her heart and then lower to the parts of her that hadn't opened themselves to a man in too many years. Why did he have to be so damn determined to know the truth? If she told him, she ran the chance of him thinking she'd lost it, but if she didn't tell him, he'd find fifty different ways to ask the same question until she answered.

"I have a database of owners with the same brand ATV as we were driving that day who also had accidents. Everyone was told that the wheel had sheared off the front axle. Every single one of them was going over thirty on the machine. There has been every imaginable injury you can think of as a result."

"And you're investigating with the working theory that the company knew what?"

"They knew the wheels would shear off the axle at higher rates of speed. And even after they found out, they continued to make and sell the machines without fixing the problem."

"That's a pretty big accusation, Kenley."

"That's why I haven't gone public with it. I'll be vulnerable and admit you're the first person I've ever told. While I know that people are still being hurt and killed by the Neo Chase, if I can't find evidence that the company knows about it, then there's no way to start a class action lawsuit."

"But there is," he said, turning slightly to make eye contact. "That's the lawyer's job to find the evidence. The legal way."

"This isn't my first rodeo, Jude. When my white hat goes dark, I get things done. I've found evidence on over thirty cases to bring people, my people, closure and justice."

Jude sat up and rubbed the sleep from his eyes. "Wait, you use the dark web to hack into companies' private files?"

"Not always," she answered, and his shoulders relaxed slightly. "Sometimes I do it on the regular web."

"Kenley!" His voice was exasperated, and she sensed a bit of disappointment. "That's vigilantism!"

"That's right!" she exclaimed, sitting up and sticking a finger in his chest. "And it gets the job done, so don't tell me it's wrong. I do it for the right reasons, and that's what matters!"

Jude sat shaking his head as she flopped onto the pillow, anger vibrating through her tightly as she forced her hands out of the fists she'd made. "I understand why you do it, Kenley. I understand you want to right the wrongs you think you've made, but you can't keep putting yourself at risk like this. Not to mention, your life isn't your own if you spend all your time in the past."

"Gabby's life passed her by, too, didn't it, Jude? She was gone before she could live! I do this for her. Every person I get justice for is also a little bit of justice for Gabby! Can't you understand that?"

"What about you? Haven't you paid a heavy enough price for a decision you didn't make? Sure, you asked her to go out, but you weren't the one running the throttle full bore. You weren't the one not listening to someone telling you to slow down. That was all her, and you can't take responsibility for her actions."

"Have you ever lost someone, Jude?" It was the only question she could think to ask that he might understand.

"Many people, Kenley. I was in the service. I'm responsible for people losing their lives."

"How do you cope with that? I'd sure like to know."

He sat in silence, his jaw ticking as he held her gaze, refusing to let it go but also refusing to answer her question. "How did you really find the Spiderweb site? Were you snooping through case files?"

"I didn't lie about that, Jude. Staun Bril, the company that makes the Neo Chase ATV, has a log of case information regarding their machines on the dark web. The only way to get to it is by typing in the fifty-two-character address. I mixed up two numbers, and the Spiderweb site popped up."

"A company has documents with dot-onion suffixes?"

"No, it's an I2P domain suffix."

"An invisible internet project? That means they're sharing it back and forth between people."

"Yep," she agreed, turning to her other side. "Since I intended to go to a different I2P domain but landed on the Spiderweb site, it makes me wonder if it also shares info between people. If that's the case, we must shut it down before it gets out of hand."

"Unless it's a government site."

"It reads like government coding, but something is off. I can't put my finger on it, but I will as soon as we get going." She glanced at the clock and blew out a breath. "It's eight p.m. We need to make some headway tonight." She sat up and stretched, dropping her arms back to the bed with a sigh. "After we eat. I'm starving."

"Me, too," he whispered right before he grabbed the front of her shirt and dragged her to him, his lips landing on hers. The emotion behind it shocked her, and she jolted. He paused the kiss until he was sure she wanted it. Rather than pull away, she tipped her head to the side and dropped her jaw, inviting him to take the kiss as far as he wanted.

Jude's kiss was hot, sweet, plaintive and moan-worthy, all in the first three seconds. Time warped, and her other senses dulled while she was under the skilled lips, tongue and hands of this man who was eight years her senior but made her feel like he was her other half. The half she'd been missing her whole life. That was a bold statement, but this was a bold kiss, and she needed to be honest with herself. She was developing feelings for Jude Mason that had nothing to do with the case and everything to do with the virile man that he was. This kiss was an accumulation of desire, need and want that had built up over the last few days. They needed an outlet for the sexually charged environment they'd been sharing.

When he ended the kiss and drew back, Kenley immediately felt lonely and filled with pain again. His lips had stolen those feelings and allowed her to feel something else for the first time in seventeen years. Something other than guilt that she lived, shame that she didn't want to, and unrelenting pain in her leg that reminded her every moment of the day she had made her bed and the knowledge that she would lie in it forever. She was torn between two worlds, the past and the present, but no matter what choice she made, someone lost. That made it an impossible choice. If there was one thing she knew for sure, it was that. She'd spent the last seventeen years trying to make the choice by not making the choice.

"Kenley," he whispered, her head in his hands as he smoothed her hair away from her face. "Why am I so drawn to you?"

"If I knew, I'd share that answer with myself," she said with a lopsided grin. "But that kiss was wow."

"Trust me, I wanted it to be so much more, but you need to hit the keys." He let his hands slide down her arms to take her hands in his. "Promise me when this is over, you'll think about finding a way to live again?"

"I can't stop helping people, Jude. That's just who I am, like it or not."

"I like it, Kenley. Don't think for a moment that I'm not impressed with your fortitude, kindness and desire to right wrongs. All I want is for you to be safe while doing it. This isn't safe."

Moved by his plea, she trailed a finger down his cheek. The shrouded room made her brave enough to open her soul to the man before her. "How many people, Jude?"

"Unfathomable numbers, sweet pea." His answer, while short, was honest to her ears.

"Is this work you do to avenge them or yourself?"

"Oh, sweet pea, it can always be both." Before she could respond, he stood and turned on the bedside lamp. "Wait there. I want to check your limb and bandage the blister before you get up. Then I'll fix some food while you get ready to work."

And like that, Jude, the man who had kissed her with an uncompromised passion, was gone, replaced by the Secure Watch operative who was ready to slay dragons for her and all of humanity. As he tenderly bandaged her limb to prepare her for the workday, she couldn't help but wish they were locked in this hotel room for a different reason at a different time with a different objective. When his eyes softened, and his hand caressed her face, she could almost convince herself they could be more someday. But wishing never got a girl anywhere. Relying on someone never got the job done in the end, either. She had to save herself and prove she wasn't a damsel in distress.

When this job is done, will your penance be paid?

Kenley shifted on the bed and shook her head at that voice.

Never.

Chapter Fifteen

The room was small, but Jude needed an outlet for his nervous energy, so he paced the short distance between the walls with his notebook in hand in case she called anything out for him to write down. Was he nervous? Yes. He was nervous that the new machine would be tracked and that they wouldn't be able to find the answers before Spiderweb went viral and took over every camera in the nation. Hell, maybe even the world. They had no idea how deep the web was woven, and he was considering a new plan. If Kenley couldn't get anything tonight, he'd burn the machines, leave them in the room and get her to Secure Watch ASAP. Once there, she could work with the team where the machines could be monitored, and more hackers could be trying to break the code simultaneously. He had no other move but that right now.

Kenley would hate that plan, but somehow, he'd have to convince her. As long as they were isolated, not only were they sitting ducks, but close contact with Secure Watch was nearly impossible. Even using the video linkup was a waiting game as Mina worked things out in the background to help them get answers. The picture, in general, was one he wanted off his wall, but to do that, he had to trust Kenley, even knowing her motivation. His steps faltered. Were her motivations significantly different than his own?

He had become a digital private investigator to do the same thing. The only difference was in how they did it. He stayed above the line while she dipped below it, at risk to herself, but to ease someone else's pain. Did that make him better than her because he kept his hat pristine? The other question he had to ask himself was, were her tactics legal? Technically, they weren't illegal, even if they were in the gray area. She wasn't breaking the law using the dark web, and from what she told him, she worked with law enforcement and the government, presumably Homeland Security, to do her part in keeping ahead of traffickers of humans and drugs. For every action, there was an equal and opposite reaction. She was thrusting her feelings of guilt onto those who truly deserved it, and the result was feeling free for a brief moment in time. At least, that was the best he could deduce from what she'd shared with him.

Telling her she shouldn't feel guilty for surviving the accident was wasted breath, he knew. He still did it as a gentle reminder that others recognized it wasn't her fault. She'd lived with this guilt for so many years it wasn't guilt anymore. It was PTSD. He'd seen it many times over in soldiers who returned from war. Hell, Lucas Porter, Delilah's new husband, struggled with the same kind of guilt. He'd been in a Humvee when it hit an IED; men on each side of him had died while he survived. There was never any rhyme or reason to death, at least not one that the living could discern. Gabby had died while Kenley lost her foot, but the tables could have been easily turned if just one factor had been different that day. If they had been in a different place on the trail, if Kenley had been sitting differently, or Gabby had hit the brakes instead of the gas, their entire life paths would have changed.

Jude crossed his arms and stared at the woman furiously typing on the laptop. What if she'd died that day? Would Gabby be doing the same thing Kenley was to try to save the world? Would Gabby try to save soul after soul after soul to atone for the loss of her friend? He couldn't know for sure, but he suspected the answer was no. Not in the way Kenley had, because everyone reacted to trauma differently. Watching Kenley so absorbed in her work that nothing else mattered did tell him more about her than her words. She cared. She loved. She hurt. She wanted to change the world. Her way of doing it just looked different than his.

It was his job to protect her, and there was a gnawing fear in his stomach that if he failed and she disappeared from his life, he would never be the same. They were here in this hotel room for a reason that had begun—

He paused as he did the math in his head. Hell, her accident had happened the same week he walked into cybersecurity school. A shiver racked him at the thought. Had he been preparing for this moment since that day? Had his career trajectory and life been aimed at 11:00 p.m. on Wednesday, October 24? Were his blood, sweat and tears over the past seventeen years all for her? Suddenly, all those choices he'd made over the years when he wasn't sure they were right came into focus, and the bigger picture was revealed. Kenley was the finished masterpiece.

"Write this down," Kenley called, and Jude snapped to attention. "If the file ends with open parentheses, open quotation dot txt close quotation close parentheses."

Her fingers flew across the keyboard, but she stopped talking, so he looked at what he wrote. "That's Python."

"Yep," she said, still typing as though her hands were independent of the rest of her body. "Send that to Mina. Ask if I'm correct that it's a prompt to search for dot txt extensions."

"On it," he promised, grabbing the phone and sending Mina an opening message. She responded immediately, and he sent the message he'd written. "Mina says, that's correct. She wants to know if that's in the program."

"Tell her yes. I've seen many of them, which tells me two things."

"Do you want me to type this to Mina?" he asked, and she nodded as she continued to work.

"Python is an AI language, so they've set the program up to work in the background anytime someone stumbles upon it. It also tells me they set it up to check directories. If it can check directories, it can infiltrate them with malware, giving them control of the camera without the owner knowing."

Frustrated with how quickly things were changing, he deleted the beginning of the message and instead sent, Will be in contact shortly. Too much to type.

"Are you saying the camera owner doesn't realize malware has been installed?"

"Essentially," she agreed with a nod of her head. "The program doesn't need to move the camera. It just needs the data it's sending back to the server mainframe."

"That's a good point." Jude let a curse word fly when the implications settled across his shoulders. "They'll use all of that information to keep training the machine so it can use it at a later date."

"Bingo," she said, still typing. "And the first thing they did was train it to block out hackers. I've busted my way through to the code without clicking any spiders, but it wasn't easy or for the faint of heart."

"I don't know many hackers this dedicated to breaking into a program." Jude only knew one, and she was sitting at an old cigarette-burned table on a subpar computer, still getting the job done.

The room went silent again, and she continued typing as code scrolled across the screen. Jude texted Mina back that she was still working. Then, he went to the kitchen and grabbed a can of Diet Coke. He was glad he'd insisted they buy snacks and drinks at the store so they didn't have to leave the room more than necessary. His mind drifted back to the moment in the condom aisle when her eyes grew to the size of saucers as he sorted through the options. He smiled. Then he remembered how she felt in his arms as he held her. Soft, sweet and perfectly fit to his body so he could protect her from harm.

Admitting that was scary. He wasn't the kind of person who needed anyone, or even desperately wanted anyone. He had to ask himself if that was because he hadn't found the right someone yet. When he and Kenley were together, the years between them melted away, and they were equals. They played off each other's strengths when the moment mattered and compensated for each other's weaknesses when time was short. He was used to a solitary work environment and life, and spending so much time with her should have felt off, but it didn't.

It felt right.

Those were the three words he'd been trying to avoid agreeing to in his head. No matter how right it felt, they had jobs in different states when they finished with Spi-derweb. The distance wasn't far, but it was far enough that a long-distance relationship wouldn't last. Then, there was the age gap to consider. Was an eight-year difference too much? Did he care? He'd enter his forties when she was still firmly planted in her thirties. Would they want different things at different times of their lives? He knew what he wanted, and that was someone to come home to every night. Someone to spend quiet nights with and share endless summer days on the lake with him. When he thought about those days, Kenley appeared beside him in every scenario. She was there saying *I do*, playing in the surf on their honeymoon and holding his baby. Kenley was there for all of it.

She had eroded his long-held belief about his life in a matter of days.

That kind of life wasn't right for a man like him.

Kenley had walked into his life and challenged a be-lief he'd held dear for over eighteen years. Was it maturity that had turned the tables on him, or was it the woman? Maybe it was a bit of both, but before he could even con-sider making Kenley a more permanent part of his life, he had to get her through this crisis. Once they were safe, he'd have to explore her feelings on the matter. She sensed the draw between them; there was no question, but that didn't mean she was looking for any kind of relationship. She didn't seem to want anything other than to be a vigi-lante for justice, however misguided that may be.

Sighing, he set the drink down and walked over to Kenley. "How's it going?" He massaged her tight shoul-ders, which resulted from hours spent on the keyboard.

"Still haven't gotten much more out of it. I saved a couple of lines of code to send to Mina to get her take on it."

"You're nearing the thirty-minute mark. Maybe you should back out now?"

"I hate to, but I think you're right. I want to wipe and restart the machine to see if it bricks."

"Do you think the program is going to install malware?"

"I hope not, but everything is on the table when dealing with machine learning."

Jude pulled up a chair and sat. "Before you sign off the dark side, are there any forums Savant visits regularly? Is there any place he might message you if you aren't responding on your phone?"

"Savant is everywhere and nowhere. I tend to stay incognito unless I'm working on a case. I burned the forum from the other night where he contacted me—at least, I'm assuming it was him, so I can't go back there. There's only one forum where I have any presence at all times. I've never seen him there, but I can check." She clicked the mouse and typed in an address, then hit Enter.

"You're a moderator of this forum?" His brow was raised to his hairline. He was not only surprised but a little bit disappointed.

"Yes, because I started it," she said with a shrug. "It's the only way to discuss some of these companies without the information being leaked."

"This is where you find your cases to solve, so to speak?"

"No, this forum is only for people who have been hurt or lost loved ones to a Staun Bril ATV."

He flicked his gaze to the number of members in the

forum and sucked in a breath of surprise. "There are over four thousand people in this forum."

"Yep," she agreed as though that was common knowledge.

"Kenley, a class action lawsuit of this size would be a no-brainer for any lawyer. Why aren't you convincing these people that's the way to get a settlement?"

The way she turned slowly in her chair said he was about to be schooled. "We don't want a settlement, Jude. That's not why we're here. We want action. We want them to stop making these ATVs. We want to avenge our loved ones and hold them responsible for our injuries. None of this is about money, don't you see that?"

He tucked a loose lock of hair back behind her ear before he spoke. "I understand that, sweet pea. This is about justice and holding the guilty parties responsible. A class action suit would do that. They'd be found guilty, but you'd also get money to take care of your prosthetic needs for years to come. It's noble that you want to shoulder this burden yourself, but you don't have to. Don't you see that?"

Rather than respond, she clicked around on the screen until she was inside a chat room, scrolling through the messages so quickly he couldn't even catch more than a word here and there. Finally, at the bottom was a private message tab. There was a notification that said 3.

"I just checked this the other night," she said with a frown before she clicked the inbox. After a quick scroll, she shook her head. "They're all from Savant."

"Is that the same account that messaged you Wednesday night?" Jude asked, and she nodded. "Which means he knows where you are."

"As I said, Savant is everywhere."

Her teeth ground together as she spoke, and he stroked her jaw tenderly. "Relax, Kenley. We aren't going to let him get the best of us. It's two against one now."

She relaxed her jaw the longer he stroked it. Her eyes closed, and she sucked in a deep breath before she clicked the first message. Once again, it was filled with 0s and 1s. "This is going to take forever."

He smiled at her grumpiness as she called up a decoder. As far as he was concerned, they had all the time in the world, and he was here for every second he could get before she disappeared from his life for good. He grabbed the phone and opened the camera.

"What are you doing?" she asked, pasting in the first message to the decoder.

"I'm saving you time. I'll take a picture of the messages so we can send them to Mina. Ready?"

With a nod, she hit Enter and the message that popped up told him they were in for a long haul. "Kenley, Kenley, Kenley. You've been a naughty girl. I think it's time I expose what you're doing and let the world pass judgment. What say you?" Jude read.

Slowly, Kenley stood, walked into the bathroom and slammed the door. When she didn't return, he slid over and got to work.

Chapter Sixteen

There was a knock on the door. "Kenley. You can't stay in there all day."

Sighing, she pushed herself up and opened the door. "Can't a girl have an existential crisis alone?"

"Not when I'm around."

"Clearly." She said the word with total and utter frustration as she walked past him into the main room.

"I decoded the other two messages, wiped the computer and rebooted it," Jude said as he grabbed a pop from the fridge and handed it to her. "Sorry, I don't have anything stronger."

She popped the top and took a long swallow. "That's okay. I don't drink. Never been my thing."

"Mine either," he agreed, lowering himself to the chair by the table while she perched on the bed. "Anyway, the computer didn't brick, which is good. I was able to do a clean install of the operating system."

"What did the other messages say?" she asked, tapping the can with her finger.

Jude grabbed the phone and opened the photo app. "The one said, Hey, bestie. Did I scare you with my last message? Yes? Good. I'm coming for you, and you won't see me until it's already done."

"What's already done?" Kenley asked, tipping her head to the side.

"I can only assume he means destroying your business, as he mentioned in the text he sent to your phone."

"Let him," she said with a shrug. "I don't even care anymore. There are far bigger problems in the world than what happens to my business. Like some terrorist having control of every camera in the world."

"Agreed," Jude said. "That's one of the reasons I shut my business down and went to work for Secure Watch—security in numbers."

"Not to mention the power of the hive mind. Okay, hit me with the third message."

"The third one was sent not long before you started working today. All it said was, Come out and play, Kenley! This is getting boring. I think he's angry that you're not engaging."

"Good. Let him focus on that. I want to get to the bottom of Spiderweb before he rears his ugly head again. I'll go back into the program while you search to see if Savant has outed me yet."

"Why do you want to go back in? It's only been an hour."

"Exactly the reason," she said, pushing herself off the bed and walking to the table. "If this is machine learning, then I would expect the path I used to get in last time to be blocked."

"The machine is anticipating the next *attack*," he said, using air quotes around attack.

"Essentially. If that bears out, then we can contact Mina and give her an update."

"Tell me more about the search you want me to do. Do

you expect him to out you, and if he were to do that, how would I search for it?"

"I don't know if he'll out me for sure, but something tells me if I make him wait too long before I engage with him again, he will. Or at least he'll try. While in the bathroom, trying not to crawl out of my skin with anger, I realized that he found the forum I had started. That means he got the address somehow, and that's why he thinks I've been a 'naughty girl.'"

Jude nodded along as she spoke. "You want me to do a dive and see if you're showing up on aboveground forums about vigilantes or a sudden flood of negative reviews for your business?"

A finger gun and a wink revealed her agreement. "My hope is he has a bit more patience in him. Just enough for me to sort the Spiderweb program and then turn it over to the cops. I'll deal with him when that's done."

"You won't be dealing with him without me," Jude said, grabbing the laptop. "Fair warning. I won't leave you alone when you're at risk for an attack. He's already been too close to you as far as I'm concerned, and he will not get close to you again."

"Jude," she said, but he held up his hand.

"Don't tell me that you're not my responsibility. I know that. You are so much more than my responsibility, so until the threats cease, or Savant shows himself, you're never alone. Understood?" When she nodded, he smiled and softened his intensity as he grabbed the phone again. "Mina is on standby right now. I'll text her to say you're conducting an experiment, and then we'll contact her."

"Thanks, Jude," she said, smiling at him. "Without you,

I'd be in serious trouble. I don't like to be a damsel, but if I have to be one, I'm glad you're rescuing me."

"No, sweet pea," he said, setting the laptop down and walking over to her. "You're not a damsel, and I'm not rescuing you. You're a brilliant, beautiful brainiac who wants to save the world. I'm here to do any heavy lifting, that's all. This is all you."

Then he leaned down and kissed her so gently her heart thumped hard in her chest. This man was doing things to her that no man ever had before. It terrified and ener-gized her at the same time. She wanted Spiderweb and Savant out of her life, but the last thing she wanted was to lose Jude, too. He ended the kiss with a caress to her cheek, and she vowed to dig deep and not stop until she found the answers they needed to cut down the spider-web and be free.

KENLEY WASN'T SURPRISED when she couldn't hack into the Spiderweb program like she had just hours before. But she was anticipating it, so it only took half as long as the last time before she waltzed through that door to inspect the code again. Mina had texted them back that while the code looked like the government created it, it was written that way to throw people off on purpose, as they all ex-pected. Kenley wanted to find the code's weakness and rid the world of this nonsense. The problem was that she would never be as fast as the machine, so trying to bust the code was impossible.

"This is just not working," she moaned, trying to keep up with the scrolling code. She finally dropped her hands to her lap to take a break. "If anything, I'm training the damn machine to be smarter and faster." Rather than give up, she put her hands back on the keyboard and clicked out of her text box, letting the code run freely across the screen, reading it as it went. "Maybe the key is finding the right place to put the code to corrupt it," she pondered.

"Is it possible you can't corrupt it from the outside?" Jude asked from across the table.

"I've never seen a program that can't be corrupted with a virus or malware."

"Have you ever seen a program like this before?"

That question didn't justify an answer since he already knew she hadn't. This program was something out of science fiction. If she had to guess, it had taken years to write the code. A 5 caught her eye, and then she realized six lines later there was another 5. She quickly took a screenshot of a code block, scanning it repeatedly for a pattern that went with the 5. Then she saw it.

"No, no," she whispered, clicking the box out and grabbing another portion of the code farther down. This time, the name screamed its presence from the page. "It can't be. It's just not possible." Her whispered denials brought Jude around the table to see what she was looking at.

Her finger shaking, she pointed out what had been there all along. "5, 4, V, 4, N, T," she read, turning to look up at the man she had come to care too much about in too short a time.

"Savant." He said the word with a finality that sat heavily in her gut. "This is Savant's work? Is he trying to prove his prowess?"

"I don't know what he's doing, Jude. He hates the government with a burning passion, though. If you go on any forum that deals with anything government-related, he'll be there shouting about the corrupt and immoral leadership in our government at every level."

"Is the government aware of this?"

"Absolutely. They've been trying to figure out where he is, but he disappears every time they get close. When he feels safe again, he pops back up."

"You mean the government doesn't know who he is?"

"Nope, at least not as of my last government job a few months ago."

"What kind of work do you do for the government, or am I not allowed to ask?"

"Let's just say I'm always on the side of the good guys, and it usually involves trafficking or drugs. We'll leave it at that." He put his hands up as if to say, *Good enough.*

"This is bad, Jude." She turned back to the program and started clicking out of it. "If Savant wrote this program, there's no hope of breaking it. I'm good, but I'm not that good. There's no one that good other than Savant."

"Do you think he knows it's you in the program?"

She shook her head back and forth a few times and finally gave him the palms up. "I can't say yes, but the fact that he made the website so close to the one I visited all the time makes me wonder if he wanted me to see it. If he hoped that eventually, I'd type something wrong and land on the page."

"Which is exactly what happened. I think you should message him," Jude said, pulling his chair over and sitting.

"Message Savant? Why?"

"He's messaged you, and you haven't responded yet, so let's give him a little attention. Make him think you're worried about your reputation, so you're distracted and scrambling."

"And unaware that he's behind Spiderweb?"

"For now, yes."

"And for later?" she asked, clicking open a tab to go to her survivors' forum.

"Later, we'll have a plan put together by one Mina Jacobs and hit him when he least expects it."

With a grin, she opened a binary code writer and prepared to type. "I like the way you think, Mr. Mason. Let's do this."

As she typed the message into the box, her head spun. Had Savant figured out a way to take control of every camera in the world? They were in serious trouble if he had, and it would be up to her and Secure Watch to stop him. Her biggest fear was that it was already too late.

Chapter Seventeen

"This guy is on every government watch list," Cal said as he walked behind Mina. "How do we find him?"

"We don't," Kenley answered. "He's been a ghost for years. I only know he's in the country because of the tracker in my shoe. For all I know, he was one of the guys in that truck tailing us. I picture him as the anonymous dude with the mask and the black robe in a dark room, staring at the camera. He may be a savant, but it's not with social skills. On the other hand, his hacking and coding skills make him the best in the world."

"Why did you decide to tangle with him?" Mina asked as she typed on her computer.

"I didn't even know who he was in the beginning," she admitted, glancing at Jude, who nodded with a smile. It felt foreign to her that, in such a short time, he was the one she looked to for strength now. Strength to keep going and the strength to say aloud the things she'd kept hidden for so many years. "I was seventeen when I started dabbling on the dark web."

"What were you looking for?" Cal asked, leaning on the back of Mina's chair. He'd joined their meeting once they knew who was behind Spiderweb. "Trouble?"

"You don't need to look for that on the dark web," Kenley said with a lip tilt. "No, I was looking for evidence that my friend's death wasn't an accident. It didn't take long to discover I was right, and thousands of people were hurt by the Neo Chase ATV, which was what my friend and I were riding that day. One second, we were flying down the trail, and the next second, we were in the dirt. She was dead, and my foot was mutilated. Over the years, I've searched for evidence to prove the company knew the wheels sheared off the axle at high speed."

"That's all you were doing there?" Mina asked, her brow tugged down to her nose in disbelief. As a former FBI agent, she knew what went down on the dark web.

"Not all," Kenley admitted, shifting in her chair. Jude put his arm around her waist and snugged her against his hip.

"Tell them everything so we can make a plan to get Savant out of our lives," Jude encouraged her.

"What he said," Mina added with a smile.

"We're not judging you, Kenley," Cal said as he pulled out a chair and sat down. "Both Mina and I have done some pretty sketchy things in the name of helping people. If that's all you were doing, you have nothing to fear."

"Not exactly true," she disagreed. "I mean, all my interactions there were for good, but I do have something to fear, and that something is someone. When Savant got wind of what I was doing, it put me on his radar."

"And what were you doing?" Cal asked, leaving the question open-ended for her to fill in.

"I worked with Mina's former employer a time or two, along with the CIA, Homeland Security, and some smaller government organizations, to help facilitate the downfall of some trafficking rings and the like. I can't say much more than that."

"And when you weren't helping mankind?" Cal asked, clearly unimpressed by her good deeds.

"I still helped mankind, but I used different techniques. I worked for individuals who were injured or had lost loved ones because of failures by large corporations. Using the dark web to find the information is the means to an end for me. Some wouldn't consider it honorable, but it's important to hold these companies accountable for their failures. It wasn't all on the dark web. A lot of that was done in the light."

"When did Savant become a problem for you?" Mina asked. "How long has he been a problem?"

"We've been sparring probably close to ten years now. He seems to have an odd fascination with me. It's like I'm his nemesis because I'm using the dark web for good and reporting those who are breaking the law."

"I'm just happy to hear that your heart was in the right place," Cal said with a wink. "I can respect someone who wants to help others even if they're motivated by their own pain."

"That sums it up pretty well," Kenley agreed. "Unfortunately, I picked up a rather unsavory character along the way, which has led us here."

"Do you think he intended for you to find the Spiderweb site?" Mina asked, folding her hands on the table and leaning in. "Otherwise, it seems like a massive coincidence."

"Agreed," Jude said as Kenley nodded.

"Now that I know he wrote the program, I can assure you, he wanted me to find it," Kenley said. "The site was set up with the same URL as the I2P page I frequented for a Staun Bril document. If he knew that, which, as the world's best hacker, he did, then all he had to do was make his URL something close and wait for me to mistype and land on it."

"Feels like there are easier ways to get you to click on his site," Jude said. "Forums and sites like that live for that kind of stuff."

"True, but I don't think he wanted anyone else to find it," Kenley said.

"You think he wanted only you to find it? To what end?"

Kenley's shrug was lazy. "My guess would be to prove he was better than me. To prove I couldn't hack his program or play with his coding. At the same time, he didn't want to take a chance that someone else might come along and report it."

"You're saying he built that entire website to prove to a woman he's better than her?" Cal asked with a hint of shock in his voice.

"Come on, Cal. You can't be surprised by that," Jude said, shaking his head. "You were in the military."

"Fair point. But now that we know this, how do we stop it?"

"I sent him a message before we called you," Kenley explained. "I told him we figured out he was the one who coded the site, and then I told him to take it down so it didn't fall into the wrong hands. I promised to leave the dark web and never return if he did."

"Do you think he's going to?" Mina asked with surprise written all over her face.

"Absolutely not," Jude jumped in. "There's no way he

spent all that time on a website with the potential to give him all this power to take it down now. I don't think this was ever really a game for him. It was, in a way, but he wanted one of the best hackers in the world to find it and try to bring it down. Savant knew he had a winning hand if Kenley couldn't take out Spiderweb. Considering how much he seems to hate the government, this entire situation was a setup to assure him he'd found a way to bring it to its knees."

"I don't disagree," Cal said, glancing at Mina, who nodded.

"I don't either," Kenley said, ignoring Jude for interrupting her. "My gut says he will return with another game. He'll give me some hints on how to get back into the program and change the code, but I won't bother. The program uses machine learning, and that's not something a human mind can ever get ahead of or beat."

"We're at a crossroads then," Cal said. "What's left to try?"

"Finding the server that holds Spiderweb." Kenley dropped the bomb without glancing at Jude. She'd purposely pretended she didn't know what to do so he couldn't talk her out of it before she got Mina and Cal on board. "If I can get to that server and install malicious firmware to the normal updating tools, then when I reboot it, it will brick the entire system."

Cal glanced at Mina. "Would that work?"

"Absolutely," Mina said, wearing a grin. "I'm sure he has the entire program backed up somewhere, but it would buy the government time to find him and stop him for good."

"Has there been any chatter about this program any-where, Mina?" Jude asked, and she shook her head.

"Nothing. No one in my government channels had heard of a program with that ability, but they were all freaked out by the concept."

"I'm more than freaked out," Kenley said. "After being inside the program, I'm terrified of what could happen if this fell into the wrong hands. I've seen enough of the code that when this is all said and done, I want to help write a firmware update that can be sent to the cameras' operating systems. That way, even if he gets the program back online, he can't get back into them."

"I can get you in touch with the right people," Mina said with a nod. "That is if your contacts can't help." She added a wink, and Kenley realized it had just dawned on them all that she wasn't just a cybersecurity professional running a business from her home.

"First, we have to stop Savant," Jude said. "How do we find that server? It could be anywhere—it could be in his mother's basement, for all we know."

Mina cracked a smile, which made Kenley chuckle.

"That's fair, but it's not. This program needs a large server—far bigger than anything he can keep in his house, much less maintain. It needs serious power with its ca-pabilities to keep changing and building in real time."

"We're back to how do we find that server," Cal said.

"We get him talking," Kenley mused. "I've started the conversation, and now he won't be able to stop bragging. Once he thinks he's defeated me, he'll give me all the in-formation I need."

"How can we help?" Mina asked.

"Get a security team together," Jude answered without pause. "If she's going in somewhere, she's not going in alone."

"Agreed," Cal said. "Once you know where the server is located, I'll dispatch a team to cover you. I'll also alert the proper authorities."

"No!" Kenley exclaimed.

Cal shook his head. "That has to be part of the deal, Kenley. We won't notify them until you're nearly done with the installation. We don't need the authorities mucking up the job, but we also have to cover ourselves legally."

Kenley let out a breath and nodded. "Okay, I can accept that. I'm glad we're on the same page. Unfortunately, it's a waiting game now. We'll give Savant time to get comfortable with my admission that I can't break his code, which will require more messages back and forth before that happens. Once it does, things should unfold quickly."

"In the meantime, we're going to eat and rest," Jude said, putting his arm around her again.

"We'll be ready when the time comes, and we'll be in touch. Secure Watch, out," Mina said, and the screen went black.

Kenley blew out a breath and stood, rolling her shoulders to ease the strain and fatigue. After pacing for a bit, she sat on the edge of the bed. "I hate the waiting game."

"Me, too, but we'll ue it to our advantage this time. I also want to check that blister in case we need a different plan."

"It's better. I'll leave the bandage on it, and in a few days, it will be nothing but a memory."

"As long as we can avoid too much walking, which might be hard depending on where the server is."

"We'll meet that challenge when we come to it. You

were working on looking to see if Savant outed me before Mina called, right?" He nodded. "Has he?"

"Not from the quick search I did of the regular web. I can't say what he did on the dark web. I'm not a pro at navigating it."

"The way I am, you mean." She didn't intend the sentence to be snarky, but it was there and chock-full of sarcasm. "You think what I do there is wrong. I suppose the rest of the world will, too."

"The more I've thought about it, the more I see why you do it," he said with a shrug. "In a way, we aren't that different. I took digital private investigation cases for the sole reason of rescuing someone in a bad situation. I can't judge what you do or how you do it if the information you need is located in a different place. If I thought for a second you were doing something that put others in danger, I wouldn't condone it, but that's not what's happening. If anything, the only person in danger is you. I wouldn't say I like that, but you're a big girl. You make your own decisions."

"Thank you for saying that, Jude." She folded her hands in a prayer pose. "I don't think it's wrong to help people any way you can, but I'm tired. I'm tired of running, hiding and playing games. I've been doing this for years, but Savant has opened my eyes to the danger I put myself in every time I go down that dark hole."

Jude stood and walked over to her, taking her hands in his. "It's good that you've come to that realization. We might take down Savant, but someone else will replace him. Fighting for justice is noble, but doing it in a way that protects you is the smartest option."

"That's what you do, right? You protect damsels in distress?" Once again, her tone was snarky while not meant to be. He was too close, too potent, and too kind, caring and handsome for her not to want to pull him to her. At the same time, the other half wanted to push him away. The battle within her was raging, and she had no idea who would win.

"Not always," he said, kneeling before her now. "At least not since I started working for Secure Watch. When I was a digital private investigator, there were many times that I was fighting for a woman who had been victimized by her husband or boyfriend. It wasn't about saving damsels in distress. It was about using my skills to right wrongs."

"You're saying we're not that different?" The question was asked with high skepticism because, in her book, Jude was far wiser about the world than she would ever be. That came with experience, and boy, did he have it. He'd lived through wars and made decisions that may have helped determine the fate of the nation.

"In most ways, we're the same, Kenley. You'll tell yourself that's impossible because we've lived different lives, which is true, but in the end, here we are with the same skills, both trying to rescue people whose lives have fallen apart."

She tipped her head to the side as she thought about the message he was trying to give her. He didn't think she was wrong because she used the dark web to dig up dirt on big corporations. He was scared that doing that would put her in danger. If that were the case, then the only reason he would worry about her being in danger was because he cared about her.

He pushed himself up to take her lips. "I care about

you, Kenley." The words were whispered against her lips before he kissed her again. Her soft mewl of happiness at the connection fueled him, and he ran his tongue across her closed lips, asking for entrance.

When she allowed it, he slipped his warm tongue alongside hers and rested there for a moment, wrapping her in his arms as he did so. Then he turned to sit on the bed, pulling her onto his lap.

"Kenley," he whispered, his breath warm against her neck as he kissed the hollow there. "I want you more than I want air."

"Same." She threw her head back when he started to kiss his way back up her neck to her ear, where he nipped the lobe.

"The age gap," he whispered into her ear.

"Doesn't matter," she moaned as he slid his hand up her ribs. "Not to me anyway. Does it matter to you?"

"Not even a little bit." Then his hand slipped under her shirt to run across her ribs and up her back, where he relieved her of her bra in one fluid motion.

"Is it just the forced proximity making us feel this way?" she asked, sliding her hands into his hair as he kissed across both collarbones.

His gentle laughter tickled her neck before he spoke. "Are you trying to talk me out of this?"

"I'm trying to make sure you don't have any regrets, Jude."

"My only regret would be not taking this chance to be with you, sweet pea." He leaned back and grasped her chin gently. "Do you know when I knew you were different than any other woman I'd met?" She barely shook her head, so he smiled and kissed her lips before he answered.

"The moment I heard your voice. This feeling came over me that said you would change my life, and there was an unseen force saying, get to her. Help her. Protect her. Then I laid eyes on you and wondered if I could draw the next breath. I've always believed I'd rather carry a little bit of regret for what I did do than a whole lot of it for what I didn't do."

"So you are going to regret this?"

He dipped his head and took her lips again as he rested her back against the pillows and then knelt over her, slowly unbuttoning her top. When the buttons were undone, he left her lips to kiss down her neck to the dip between her breasts. He laid his lips there for a beat before he gazed at her from his position on her chest. "The only thing I'll regret about this is that, eventually, I'll have to wrap you up again and take you back out into that cold world. For now, just for now, let's pretend we don't."

Before she could speak, he pushed aside her bra and lavished her breasts with the attention they'd been begging for. His warm hands kneaded and caressed them while his hot tongue teased her nipples into hard buds in the chilly room. With his hands still on her breasts, he kissed his way down her belly, dipping his hot tongue in her navel and pulling an unexpected gasp from her lips. She slid her hands back into his hair and pulled him up to kiss her while she worked at the buttons of his shirt. She wanted to see, touch and feel his heat and energy against her skin.

"Let me take off your prosthesis," he whispered as she ran her hands over his hard chest, the soft hair tickling her fingers. Her hands froze, and she glanced up at him, grabbing his hand as it went for her leg.

"Leave it on. It won't hurt anything."

He shrugged the rest of the way out of his shirt before he leaned in to press himself to her chest, matching their hearts together. "Absolutely not. It pains me to know you want to leave it on to protect yourself. I desire all of you, Kenley. Your leg has no bearing on that. If any other man thought your leg wasn't worthy of the same kind of attention and care as the rest of you, then he wasn't the right man."

"You mean every man, then?" she asked with her smart-aleck tone back in force. She wished she could find a place to be less defensive about her leg, but she hadn't lied when she said every man she'd been with took issue with it in one way or another. They all thought she was a little less beautiful, a little less talented, and maybe a little less everything because of it.

"All the wrong men," he said, taking her hand and kissing her knuckles. He walked to the end of the bed, his belt open, and the snap on his jeans popped. She could see the outline of his maleness and yearned to touch him, but he was a man on a mission.

Jude lifted her prosthesis and took his time removing the back plate so she could slip her limb out. He set it aside and then rolled the liner sock down, obviously having paid attention to the way she did it, and then stowed it in the prosthesis.

With unhurried tenderness, he held the end of her limb in one hand while running the other over her skin, raising goose bumps. When he lowered his lips to kiss his way up the limb to her knee, she had to swipe away a tear. His gentle caress and tender kisses did everything to heal the part of her heart that believed she was damaged and unlovable or needed to prove herself because of what was missing, not what she still had.

When his fingers grasped the waistband of her lounge pants, she lifted her bottom, allowing him to strip them off in one motion. In the blink of an eye, she was bare and open to the man who, just a few days ago, was a stranger. Not anymore. He'd become so much more the moment their eyes met, and as she watched him gaze at her body as though she was priceless art, she understood why. He was made for her.

"Beyond beautiful," he whispered, running his hand up the inside of her right thigh to her groin. "I've ached for someone like you, sweet pea, for years." The sentence was barely complete before he lowered his lips to her thigh and kissed his way to her center, teasing and sucking until she wanted to come apart from the power of his lovemaking.

"Jude," she cried, grasping his belt loop and pulling him to her. "Let me see you." Her words were laced with passion, but as he lowered his boxers, she came to understand her desire for him fully. "Let me touch you."

With a smile, he took her hand and taught her how he liked to be held, touched and tasted. When he could take no more, he climbed onto the bed and grabbed a silver packet from the drawer by the bed.

Her brow went up. "You did have plans." She snatched the packet from his hand and waved it in the air.

When he laughed, it was dirty and delicious. "I'll admit I bought a bigger box than necessary, just in case."

"Always prepared," she said, ripping open the package. "Kind of like a Boy Scout."

"Oh, sweet pea, I am the furthest thing from a Boy Scout you'll ever find."

"Good, because I like a bad boy, and I like him dirty." Before he could respond, she popped the condom between her lips and rolled it over him slowly and with precision. A moan ripped from his chest, indicating exactly how he felt about her actions.

"The good girl is about to learn how dirty this bad boy likes it," he whispered as he poised at her juncture. "And then, we'll have to review for the test."

She inhaled as he thrust forward, filling her with nothing but good sensations. When he pulled back and thrust forward again, she was struck with the need to be with this man until the end of time. His legs shook from the effort it took to hold back, so she wrapped her legs around his waist and lifted her hips. He slipped deeper, and when their eyes met, she watched him fall for the good girl, her name on his lips.

Chapter Eighteen

Jude woke to the clacking of keys, though he could tell she was trying to be quiet. The woman he'd made love to just an hour ago was wearing his T-shirt while sitting at the table, typing a message. He was taken by her before, but after sharing such intimacy, he was a goner. His only goal was to not let that show once they left this room. He couldn't risk allowing her sweet body or the idea that she could be his to distract him when he was the only one there to protect her.

Did he think Savant was still stalking them? He'd told Kenley he'd pulled back his friends, which was supposedly all in good fun, but it didn't feel like fun when they were trying to avoid that pickup truck. As for digitally, it was unlikely he had a pin on them yet. The VPN provider and scrambler they used changed their location so quickly that it was next to impossible to break through and find their actual location. Even if he knew where they were, let him come. Savant was nothing more than a bully made of flesh. Jude had dealt with plenty of them.

"Savant responded," she said without turning as though she knew he was awake. "He's hedging on my conceding the game already."

"Did he expect you to beat your head on the wall for a few more days?"

"That's what I just asked," she said, finally turning to smile at him. Her hair was mussed from his fingers, and her lips were still plump from his kisses. "I told him I'm persistent, but I'm not dumb. There's no way for me to get ahead of a machine that can compute ten times faster than I can."

"Now we're back to waiting?" he asked as she turned off the computer and stood. "Do you think he's still tracking us?"

"That was the other half of his message. He congratulated me on figuring out he was tracking the phone but was frustrated that he couldn't find the new device I was using."

The mere idea lifted Jude's lips. "Excellent. The last thing we want is to run into his goons again. He said he called them off, but there's no telling what he might do if he feels threatened and has our location."

"Agreed," Kenley said.

She walked over to him, standing between his legs where he sat on the bed. He hadn't dressed, and while his nakedness would typically make him feel vulnerable, just the opposite was true. He was confident, which was never something he felt with any other woman after sex.

Maybe the difference is you made love to Kenley.

Though that *was* probably the difference, it didn't fix any of the other circumstances they found themselves in. If anything, emotions could do more harm than good in a life-or-death situation. The problem was the emotions were there, which meant he had two choices. He could use them to his benefit or let them get the better of him.

The military worked to instill the idea that emotions didn't belong on the battlefield. If that were true, thousands of men who were saved by the sheer will and determination of another human being over the course of history would have died rather than been rescued, patched up or protected. Sometimes, you could fight evil with love. That might be what he'd have to do here if Savant came at them.

Jude grasped her hips and snugged her into him. He wanted to slide his hands under the T-shirt to connect with her tender skin. "How do you feel?"

"Satisfied. Happy. Surprised," she whispered, leaning in to kiss him as he cupped her bottom, loving the feeling of her warm skin under his hands again.

"Surprised?"

With her lips near his ear, she answered. "You're the first man who has ever been comfortable with my leg or willing to touch it, much less kiss it the way you did."

Jude suspected that was the case, but it broke his heart to have it confirmed. "Maybe those other men saw your leg as a weakness but I see it as strength. Physically and morally. It's often painful and difficult, but you keep going because you're determined to turn that pain and loss into something good that will benefit others. It takes a strong mind and body to do that, Kenley. I'm sure there were times you wanted to give up or give in, right?" She nodded against his neck, where her lips had made their way. She was kissing her way back to his ear, raising goose bumps on his skin and a more visible reaction from his groin. "But you didn't give up. You kept going through all the pain and all the grief to stand for something you believe in."

"I thought you didn't agree with my vigilantism."

"After some reflection, I understand why you do it. Though the how may not be to my liking, if you're changing lives and not breaking any laws, then I have no right to judge you. All I want is for you to be safe, and I feel like right now, you're not."

"Right now," she said, gazing into his eyes as her pupils dilated. "I've never been safer. When I'm in your arms, nothing can hurt me. I know you'll keep me safe, Jude, both physically and emotionally. Right?"

A growled yes was all he got out before she grasped him in her hand. On his surprised intake of breath, she laid a kiss on him that said emotion was in play for her, too. She might not know where they were going, but she knew they would get there together. He thrust against her hand, and a moan fell from his lips when she pulled away from the kiss. She reached into the drawer and grabbed another silver packet.

"Will you prove it?" she asked in a whisper, rolling the condom down and pushing him backward on the bed. She climbed up and straddled him, pressing her lips to his again in a desperate attempt to have as little space between them as possible.

"I'll prove it over and over and over," he promised against her lips as she lowered herself over him inch by inch until she was fully seated on his lap, his hardness throbbing at the heat and pleasure she offered but also at the trust she had put in him. The mere thought had him thrusting upward to close all the gaps of reality between them. In one fluid motion, he stripped the shirt from her tiny body and reveled in the beauty before him. "You're so damn beautiful, Kenley Bates. Don't ever take that away from me."

Before she could say anything, he grasped her nipple between his lips and suckled, bucking his hips against hers in a race to the finish line that would have them falling into each other's arms as winners. He didn't want to think about anything outside this room or this woman. He didn't want to think. He just wanted to feel, so for now, he'd pretend they were any other couple stealing away for a tryst before returning to reality.

"Jude," she moaned, her head thrown back as she stilled against him.

His name on her lips was all he needed, and he drove them across the finish line in a short thrust. She called his name one last time and fell against him, spent and sated. He wrapped his arms around her and pulled the blankets over them, loving how she settled into his chest and dropped off to sleep. After a kiss to the top of her head, he let his eyes droop closed, too, taking advantage of what little quiet time they had before the storm intensified and they were swept up into a tornado that might eat them alive.

JUDE TUCKED THE blanket around Kenley and grabbed the phone before he slid outside to stand against the door. After having her sweet body over him, he needed some fresh air to get his head back in the game. It wasn't just that they'd made love again. It was that she'd given herself to him in a way he wasn't expecting or prepared for when she straddled him. There were no declarations of feelings, but they both sensed it was more than sex between two people trapped in a situation not of their making. It was the coming together of two hearts that had finally found each other.

With a breath out, he hit the button and waited while the phone rang. "Secure Watch, Whiskey."

"Secure Watch, Jacko," he responded, and Mina's face popped up on the small screen. "Hey, Min."

"Jude, good to see you. I was hoping you'd be in touch and update me."

"About an hour ago, Kenley got a message from Savant. He's suspicious that she's thrown in the towel already. She assured him she had better things to do than try to go head-to-head with a machine that could compute ten times faster than she could. We're awaiting his response."

"Give me your opinion, Jude. What do we have here?"

"We have a dude whose brain is like a computer, but he has zero social skills that tell him when something isn't acceptable."

"Agreed. His name is fitting. He's a savant who has skills that should be harnessed by the government, not having him working against them. What do you think his endgame with the Spiderweb program is?"

"At first, I thought it was a way for him to mess with Kenley because he has so much hatred for her and what she does on the dark web."

"That's never been very clear on our end," Mina admitted.

Jude took a moment to explain in more detail what Kenley did and why. "She admits that sometimes she's looking at documents she shouldn't be, but feels like if a company is lying about a product that is hurting people, it's her job to expose them."

"And the government jobs she does?"

"To ease her guilt about the rest of it," Jude answered. "She hasn't come right out and said that, but it's the vibe

I got as we talked. When she sees something, she says something. Whether it's a sex trafficking ring, drugs or murder plot, she always lets the authorities know where to look. Sometimes, she does the looking for them."

Mina shrugged with a smile. "Maybe this makes me a bad person, but I have zero qualms with what Kenley is doing with these companies. So many of them are telling bald-faced lies to sell products that harm people. I'll take her tactics all day long if she can stop just one person from getting hurt. That said, and as I'm sure she's learned, the dark web is a dangerous place to play. I hope this event has proven that to her."

"Oh, it has," Jude agreed with a nod. "She wants to find Savant and then return to the business that makes her money and nothing else. She decided that vigilantism can only go so far."

"Too bad. Cal and I considered offering her a job at Secure Watch."

Jude raised a brow at that bomb. "Really? I didn't think Cal would condone what she does enough to trust her."

"Cal? My dude, he's spent half his life as a vigilante. He's never met her, but he feels a commonality he can respect."

"True. It's easy to forget what Cal did before Secure One grew to be so successful."

"We also see a commonality between you and Kenley."

Jude rubbed his forehead as he took in the area around him. The same bikes that had been there earlier were still parked in a row along the doors. There weren't any pickup trucks or other cars besides Blob the Slob, who was still hunkered in the spot where they parked him at the very edge of the lot. He'd decided it was better not to point the genius directly to their door if he were to show up. Jude prayed that Blob started again when they needed to leave, because there would be a showdown, even if he didn't know when or where yet.

"Jude? Care to respond?"

"If I say no, can that be the end of the discussion?"

Mina's laughter traveled through the phone and into the space around him. He couldn't help but smile even if he was extremely uncomfortable. "You should know me better than that by now, Jude Mason."

"It was worth a shot," he said with a shrug and a lip tilt. "I should get back inside and check messages. Kenley finally gave in to sleep, so I'll take this shift while she rests."

"How's her limb?"

"Healing," he answered, letting a breath out in relief that she wasn't going to keep grilling him about his feelings for the woman asleep behind the door. He might say something he shouldn't. "The last time I bandaged it, I saw new skin over the blister, and the swelling was down. She can wear her prosthesis now without pain. We must keep her off her feet as much as possible, though."

"You bandaged it?" Mina asked, surprise filling her tone.

"I did. Kenley has bad judgment when it comes to whether something is fine or in need of help. I don't have that bias."

"Fair," she agreed. "I'm just surprised she lets you touch her limb. I couldn't bring myself to let Roman touch mine for months after the amputation."

"The vulnerability was real, but we got past it and are better for it. I needed to understand her limitations in that prosthesis, so I didn't push her past them again. She says there are better ones, but she can't afford them. She never got a settlement from the accident and has to pay for everything herself."

"That's unfortunate. I hoped that wasn't the case, but I'm not surprised. So few insurances pay for prostheses. It's something that needs to change. Maybe that's my ace in the hole. She could get whatever she wanted if she worked at Secure Watch." Mina threw him a wink. He smiled at the idea that maybe there was a better, healthier path forward for Kenley.

"Do you know that she has over four thousand people on a forum who have been hurt by the same ATV that caused her accident? I've been slowly prodding her into filing a class action lawsuit. If what she says is true, a lawyer would certainly find evidence that the company knew about the problem."

"That's a lot of people. I'm surprised no one has brought a suit against them already."

"Some have, apparently, but have given up after hitting constant roadblocks. That's why they turn to Kenley. Well, anyway, you should go be with your family."

"You care about her, don't you?" Mina asked, completely ignoring his statement.

"She needs someone in this life to care about her, Mina." That was a safe answer to all the questions swirling around in his brain.

Mina's laughter was softer this time as she shook her head. "Very military diplomat of you, Jude. Here's what I'll say about the look on your face and the spark in your eye when I say her name. Over the next few days, as we try to stop Savant, use it. Don't be afraid of it. Use it to keep her safe and make the right decisions about your future."

"Use what, Mina?" Did she want him to admit he loved Kenley? It had only been a few days since they met.

"That love you feel for her." He opened his mouth to speak, but Mina held up her hand. "Don't come at me, bro. I'm simply telling you what I see. You look like a well-loved man tonight, and I'm here for it. If there's one thing I've learned in this life, it's that if you fight evil with love, you'll win every single time. You may take a few hard hits, but love will always win, so use it to your advantage to keep that woman safe. The team is ready to help, but right now, you're the only thing standing between her and Savant, so be the pillar she needs and show her how much you care even if you can't put that into words now."

"The fact that I can put it into words at this moment scares me. It's only been three days, Min. It takes me three days to decide to put away my laundry."

"Oh, Jude," Mina said with a chuckle. "You do make me laugh. Love isn't always a matter of time. Sometimes time is what brings us love."

"Change the narrative," he said.

"And change your life," she said with a wink. "I'm going to get back to digging into the government's knowledge of this program and whether they already have someone on it. Right now, all signs point to no, but I'd be surprised since Savant is very much on their radar."

"You have to remember how the dark web works, Mina. That's where you go when you don't want the government to discover what you're doing. Savant has used that to his full advantage. If he could put malware on cameras without leaving a trace, no one would be the wiser until he sells the program or uses the information for evil. Only then would they realize something was wrong."

"And by then, it would be too late." She sighed.

"We have to stop him in any way possible. That said, bringing the authorities in too early will hinder our ability to do that, no matter what Cal says. According to Kenley, Savant hates the government with the heat of ten thousand suns, which means he will continue to push back with bigger and bolder programs unless he's stopped for good."

"We agree there. Please message me as soon as you hear something from Savant. The security team is on standby until we have a plan."

"Heard and understood," he said. "Thanks, Mina. For all the advice, too."

"No thanks needed as long as you take some of it. Whiskey out."

Jude hung up the phone and let out a sigh. Was he going to take any of her advice? He unlocked the door and slid back inside, not surprised to see Kenley still asleep as the clock ticked toward midnight. The longer he gazed at her, the more he understood that Mina was right. Sometimes, time brought love. He had to agree as he walked over to the bed and caressed Kenley's cheek, bringing a smile to her lips as she slept. Now, he just had to keep that love safe until he could share it.

Chapter Nineteen

Kenley watched Jude work from her position on the bed. Funny, it was only a few hours ago that he had done the same to her, as though they were sizing each other up for how big a heartache they'd cause each other. Was it weird that she didn't want to be the cause of his heartache and just be his heart? Less than seventy-two hours wasn't a long time to get to know someone, but it had only taken the first time she saw him step out of his SUV to know she was about to meet her destiny. Maybe that sounded ridiculous, but it was the image lodged in her heart. Not because he was coming to save her either. Because he was coming at all. He could have said to take a cab home and call in the morning, but he hadn't done that. He'd driven almost two hours in the middle of the night to extract her from a place that had suddenly become dangerous.

His fingers flew across the keyboard as the adrenaline in the air caught up to her. "Jude, what's going on?"

Once she'd strapped her prosthesis back on, she grabbed her lounge clothes, slipping into them before she walked over to him. The last thing they could do was get distracted by each other again.

"Savant responded to your message," he answered quickly as he typed in a program she didn't recognize.

"We've been conversing, and he had some interesting things to say to you."

"Why didn't you wake me up?"

"You needed the sleep. It never occurred to him that it wasn't you who was answering. He was responding quickly, so I just kept the ruse up."

"Does he believe I've given up on breaking the code?"

"Oh, yeah," Jude said with a lilt of laughter at the two words. "Now he thinks he's bulletproof, and that's exactly where we want him."

"That's when he'll slip up, right?"

"He already did, sweet pea," he said, hitting Enter on the keyboard and waiting for the information to hit his screen. Jude turned to her and took her face in his hands, kissing her with a hard smack of excitement. "Pretending to be you, I asked him where Spiderweb sleeps, and he said it was a secret we'd never uncover. He also kept referring to Spiderweb as a cyclone. One that would sweep the entire world right into his hands."

"A cyclone? That's weird. We don't have cyclones in the Midwest. We have tornadoes."

"Exactly!" Jude exclaimed, turning back to the computer screen. "But Iowa State University's football team is the Cyclones."

"Are you saying he knows we're here?"

"Nope, I'm saying I think Spiderweb sleeps in Iowa. I just have to find it."

"How?"

"Well, he mentioned this professor he once had. According to him, when he was twelve, he attended college at Iowa State, and she taught him advanced coding techniques. Her name was Professor Dracker."

"Hero worship?"

"It felt a little like that. Whether that was his point or not, I can't say, but it was an odd last name. I searched Mina's databases, and there's no Professor Dracker at Iowa State, but it did bring up a former Iowa State professor who now works on Dracker Drive in Ames."

"I'm not connecting the dots."

He held up his finger and waited for the computer to finish spinning. When it did, they both sucked in a breath. "I knew it," he said, shaking his head with a smile. "He couldn't resist thinking he was so smart."

"That Spiderweb sleeps on Dracker Drive in Ames, Iowa?" She leaned in to see the screen a bit better. "Pauline Hardy is now a cybersecurity specialist for hire?"

"And it looks like she's not afraid of the underbelly of that kind of cybersecurity." He pointed out some information on the screen for her to read.

"She's listing her expertise in all things dark web scraping. That sounds like the kind of company Savant would keep. Can you bring the address up on maps?"

After opening a browser and typing in the address, they waited until the pin grabbed the location. Jude hit the street view and zoomed in to check it out. "Looks like an office building. She must rent space there."

"Does it give a suite number or anything?" He flipped back to the other tab, and she searched the page, but nothing was listed. "That's inconvenient. Do you think she owns the entire building?"

"Anything is possible. It could also be on a directory in the building."

"What if it's a trick?"

Jude tossed his head from side to side. "I considered

that. It would be easy for a guy like Savant to plant a fake name on the internet, but something tells me everything he said was true. Is he leading us to the building? That's what I believe, but maybe it's the only way this will ever end. All we can do is not take anything at face value, and both be on the same page before making a move. If something feels off, we fall back and regroup."

With a nod, she took his hand. "I agree with everything you said. If he's giving us these 'clues'—" she used air quotes "—then he wants us to find this building and whatever is inside. If we're lucky, it will be the home of Spiderweb, and we can finally exterminate it. What do you say, partner? Are you up for a short road trip?"

"I wouldn't have it any other way," he promised, kissing her firmly. "Let me call Mina while you pack. We have a date with data and destiny in Ames."

Jude grabbed the phone, and Kenley hurried to the bathroom to change her clothes and pack. When she closed the bathroom door, she realized she had never questioned Jude's deductions and didn't ask to see the messages. Jude Mason had all her trust. Now, she had to hope he didn't break it.

JUDE UPDATED CAL on their location while Kenley stood with her back against the building, waiting. The office building on Dracker Drive was much larger than she expected, and their research on it was minimal. Unfortunately, they couldn't approach the front door to look for a directory, as it faced the street and several large cameras. They'd found a door at the back that had one small camera and a keypad. Jude pulled out a can of black spray paint and contorted his arm, giving the lens a shot of the paint.

It would buy them time and not much else. Then again, there was a good chance the building didn't have anyone running security inside, and the cameras went to a security company's central hub. Kenley prayed that was the case. They needed enough time to get inside and find a server large enough to hold Spiderweb.

When they climbed into Blob the Slob to leave the hotel, Kenley had sucked in a breath on a hope and prayer that it would start. As she stood staring at the door to what could hold her destiny, she realized she hadn't let it out yet. This was far from over. They were just getting started, but fortunately, the car had started on the first try. Since Ames was less than an hour from the hotel, they made record time getting to the building.

"We have to wait for the rest of the team to arrive," Jude whispered. "They need to run interference for us. Not to mention, we can't get the door open without the right PIN. We also don't know what's inside, if there are servers, or which would be his."

"It's simple," she replied as they scooted along the building toward the keypad. If her theory were correct, she'd get the door open after one or two attempts. "He goes by 54V4N7 online. He's also arrogant and has a God complex, so I'm pretty sure I can bust his code."

"We're not supposed to go in until Cal and the team get here."

Kenley checked her watch. "They're easily another hour out, Jude. Savant could kill the program or move it off this server to a different one if we wait. He could be doing that now for all we know!"

He grasped her elbow to calm her. "If we go in and get caught, Secure Watch can't help us."

"I'll take my chances," she said, pulling the hood up on the black hoodie she'd found in her bag. "Are you with me, Warrant Officer Mason?"

"I've got your back. You get two tries. If you can't get in, we'll wait for Cal."

"Agreed," she said, sliding toward the keypad while trying to avoid the camera. He'd given it a shot of paint, but they had no way to know if a hidden camera was inside the keypad. The best she could do was shield her face with the hoodie and pray. Before she stepped up to the keypad, she checked her pocket for the flash drive she'd tucked in it before they left the car. She'd written the code for the malware while at the hotel and had it ready to install in Savant's server once they found it. A little click-clack and Spiderweb would be demolished.

After a deep breath in, Kenley inspected the keypad. She wasn't surprised it was low-end technology. It was doubtful too many people tried breaking into a random office building. While she knew it was wise to wait for the team, it was also a considerable risk that Savant would tire of the game, pack up his toys and go home. Jude might think the evil genius was being coy by dropping hints, but Kenley knew better. Savant had orchestrated this entire game. He wanted an epic showdown with her, so he made Spiderweb's address so close to the one she had always visited. He'd never made it a secret to anyone who would listen that he took offense at what she did on the dark web and wanted to bring her down. In his opinion, the dark web should never be used for good, but that wasn't an opinion they shared.

Savant must have wanted her to find the server. What would be waiting for her when she got there was impossible to predict, but she knew the time was now if she was going to beat him at his own game. All she could do was cross her fingers that he was still behind a keyboard somewhere, not behind this door. Her flash drive would solve the problem, but first, she had to find where Spiderweb slumbered.

Chapter Twenty

Kenley inhaled a breath and typed 5447 on the keypad, then waited for the door to click. When it didn't, she cleared the pad and typed in 5135. With a snap, the lock disengaged, and she pulled it open, waiting for Jude to join her.

Once inside, he pulled her against a wall and leaned into her ear. "How did you do that?"

"I suspected the code would be a combination of our call letters. It wasn't even hard, but he's cocky, so I'm not surprised."

"We are in the middle of nowhere. He probably thought he was safe from anyone bothering to try and break the code to get in," Jude said as they made their way down empty corridors. "That also means that this woman he's talking about may not exist, and this building is his."

Jude's words made her trip on her own feet. She pulled up against the wall and took a deep breath. "You're right. I didn't think of that. Why would a code specific to him open the door if someone else owned this building? Of course, he is the world's best hacker. He could have changed the pad code in anticipation of our arrival."

"He could have, but my gut says he's the owner. We need to wait for backup from Secure One, Kenley. This guy means business. You say he's a harmless nerd, but I don't feel that way. The hair on the back of my neck is standing up."

"Mine, too, but we don't have time to wait. It's been three hours since you chatted with Savant. If we don't make a move, he will."

"That's what I'm afraid of," Jude mumbled, following her as she scooted forward. She pointed at a directory listing near a set of double glass doors.

They read the list of businesses, and Kenley immediately started to sweat. "They're all names of spiders," she whispered, pointing at the directory. "Tarantula, Black Widow and Brown Recluse." When she finished reading, she stepped back and took it all in. "This one." Her finger pointed at the fifth one up.

"Sydney Funnel-Web?" Jude asked, and she nodded.

"It's the most poisonous spider in the world, and it has 'web' right in its name. It's also on the fifth floor."

"That means?"

"His name on the web starts with a 5," she clarified.

"I'll bite, no pun intended." He gave her a wink that instantly lowered her heart rate as they moved closer to their own Black Widow. "What's your plan?"

"Find an elevator," she responded, and he raised a brow. "Where there's an elevator, there are stairs."

"Fair point, but I feel like we're going deeper into the underbelly of this place."

"We are, but if we use service stairs, we're less likely to get caught on camera right away."

They walked down several more corridors before they found the elevator. Sure enough, there was also a set of stairs. As they took each flight, Jude allowed her to set the pace, and she did her best to keep from grimacing. The stairs were rough in her prosthesis but worse when she had a blister to protect. Not doing this wasn't an option. If she ever wanted to be free without looking over her shoulder, she had to stop Savant.

At the top of each flight of stairs was a heavy steel door. Jude grasped her arm and held her still halfway up the last steps to floor 5. "Catch your breath before we go any further. How's the leg doing?"

Before saying it was fine, she stopped and took stock of everything. "We're good. Your bandage is holding up." Admitting that almost choked her up. Earlier, he'd insisted they weren't leaving the hotel room until he'd assessed and rebandaged the blister on her limb. Thankfully, the last few days of lying low had helped heal it quickly and without infection. She'd get away with nothing but a memory as long as the swelling stayed down. She just had to hope all these stairs didn't worsen the problem. Then again, everything was about come to a head, which meant their days of hiding out would be over, and she could go to the doctor if needed.

Sadness filled her at the thought of giving Jude up for good. He had a life in Illinois working for Secure Watch. She had a business in Milwaukee. The miles between them weren't insurmountable, but assuming he wanted to be part of her life after all this was an assumption she couldn't let her heart entertain. They were good together at the keyboard and in bed, but did that translate to life? She couldn't answer that question, but her gut told her the moment she lost Jude, she'd feel it in her soul forever. Did it scare her that she could see a future as a couple for them in only three days? Yes, but not in the terrifyingly scary kind of way. More in the anticipation kind of scary.

"That's a relief. Let's keep it that way," he whispered, kissing her softly. "Stay right where you are." He pulled the phone from his pocket. "I have to update Cal."

"How far out are they?" she asked, trying to read the message over his shoulder.

"About ten minutes. It turns out he brought the chopper. Mina is waiting in a secure location with a computer. Once you install the malware, she'll log on to the program to see if it implodes. I'm giving Cal the credential information now because this feels like a setup to us."

Kenley bit her lip for a moment. "I was just thinking everything was a bit too easy."

He sent the message and glanced at her. "I think we should wait for the team. I have hand-to-hand skills, but that's nothing against a knife or a gun."

"I thought you had a gun?"

"I do, but the last thing I want is for bullets to start flying. If there's nowhere to hide, you could get hit."

Kenley turned and grabbed his shirt in her fists. "I care about you too, Jude. The last thing I want is for anyone to get hurt. I can go in alone. It'll take less than five minutes to plant the malware and leave."

"You are absolutely not going in there alone. We don't know who or what is waiting for us. We don't even know what we're looking for!" His voice was barely audible, but she heard the frustration and fear loud and clear.

"Savant is too smart to be dangerous to our bodies, Jude. I know him."

"I'm less worried about the evil genius and more worried about the person he hired as his muscle. If you don't believe he did, you're naive, Kenley Bates."

She shook her head momentarily before unzipping her pocket and readying the flash drive. "I believe this game of cat and mouse needs to end, Jude. For me, for you, and the world. Whatever we find in there can be weaponized to destroy countries. That's not something I want hanging over my head because I was too afraid to stop it." She shook the flash drive in her hand. "Am I scared to death? Yes. But sometimes you have to live scared, Jude, so let's do it. Let's live scared."

Before she could turn, he grasped the back of her neck and pulled her into him. When his lips landed on hers in a passionate kiss that was fast and dirty, she memorized every second of it so she wouldn't forget. "You want me to live scared? Fine, I'm frozen with fear, knowing I could lose you in the next five minutes. I'm terrified knowing that if we live through whatever is about to happen, I'll lose you when our world stops spinning on an axis created by Savant. I'm even more terrified that I'll never have a chance to tell you that I lo—"

Kenley put her finger against his lips. "Shh." It was no more than a hiss. "Do not say those three words, Jude Mason. Save them. Save them until they can mean something more than a hurried confession in a stairwell. If you say those three words, I'll take your hand and run away from all of this to be with you."

"Let's do it. Let's run away," he begged, holding her elbow. "We can let the authorities and Secure Watch deal with Savant."

"And they will, but for all we know, Savant is launching an attack with Spiderweb as we speak. Since the day

I logged on to the dark web, this was my destiny. I have to finish it. You have to trust me."

She waited while Jude stared her down, his jaw ticking as he made whatever decision he had to make. She fell even more in love with him with every moment he stayed by her side. He could turn around and walk down those stairs to wait for Cal, but she knew he wouldn't do that—not if he loved her.

"All right, but if I see one thing I don't like, we back off and wait for the team."

With a nod, she turned and finished walking up the stairs, peering through the window in the door into floor 5. "It just looks like another hallway," she said.

"I hate hallways," Jude muttered as she opened the door. They slipped through, following the long, dark corridor.

Kenley noticed it branch off to the left ahead, and she motioned Jude against the wall so she could peek around the corner. Then she leaned into his ear to fill him in. "Offices filled with nothing but servers. This is where Spiderweb is."

"How do we find the right server?"

Kenley had already considered this, and if her luck or Savant's ego held true, she knew the answer: "Fourth office, fourth rack, seventh shelf."

"His name numbers again?" When she nodded, he shrugged as though he didn't have a care in the world. "Let's try it. Maybe there will be other markings on it to tell us for certain. I don't want to crash someone else's program."

"This malware is geared to shut down Spiderweb only.

As long as no one else is trying to target all the cameras in the world, my malware wouldn't harm their program."

"Brilliant," Jude whispered, and she noticed a grin on his face.

"It's a stopgap measure until we can get the patch out to everyone with security cameras. I'm not convinced he doesn't have a backup somewhere."

"Beat him from the inside out. There's no other answer when fighting someone we can't see. Are you ready?"

He squeezed her hand, and they slid around the corner, staying tight to the wall to avoid detection as much as possible. It was dark, but the servers put off a fair amount of blue light to guide them. She mentally counted off the offices until they reached office four at the back of the building. With a nod from Jude, they slid across the hallway and into the room. Jude pushed her up against the wall and held up his finger. He drew his gun and walked around the large server cabinets, checking between each one with his gun pointed forward.

"It's clear. Fast and ugly, right?"

She nodded while he took up a shooter's stance at the door. Kenley counted seven data racks in total, so she counted four over and then seven servers down. There was a translucent spiderweb sticker over the front of the display.

"Found it," she whispered. "But the rack is locked."

"Wire cutters left side pouch," Jude said without turning to her. "Cut the cage and reach your hand in to open it."

"Well, look at you," Kenley said, grinning as she pulled the cutters out of his belt. She lifted herself on her toes and kissed his cheek. "Always the Boy Scout."

She registered his amused snort as she cut into the cabinet. After a few frantic minutes, she had a hole big enough for her arm to slip through and unlock the cabinet. She finally had access to Savant's game.

Kenley knelt and worked the server out of its slot, needing access to the back of it for the flash drive. Once she had it inserted, she needed to reboot the system, which would implode the system as a whole. While he might have a backup somewhere, she couldn't worry about that now. That was a problem for an older, more mature Kenley, who would pass her information to the government and let them deal with the evil genius.

The flash drive was cold in her palm as she gripped it, contorting herself enough to find the slot on the back of the server. Almost giddy, she slid the drive into the slot and smiled at Jude. Almost there. Savant used a headless server, meaning no monitor, keyboard, or mouse was in play. She had a keyboard in her backpack, but she hoped that if she unplugged the server, it would be enough to reboot it and bring it back online. She needed to plant this and get out, so Mina would have to tell them if the internal server destruction worked.

Kenley found the power cord and the backup power cord and pulled them both. When she pulled them, a bright light lit up the office in front of theirs. Since the rooms were glass boxes, the light was blinding. Kenley threw her arm up to her face as Jude did the same.

"You are in a tricky position, aren't you, Sickle," a voice said from the other office.

In one motion, Jude stepped in front of Kenley, who was still on the floor. He aimed the gun at the glass in front of them. "Who are you, and what do you want?"

"Let's ask Kenley who I am."

"Savant." The word dripped like poison from her lips. "Why all the games?"

"Because I like to win, Sickle."

"You're not going to win this time, Savant. People know."

"The people who know can do nothing to Spiderweb. The government couldn't work together long enough to tie a shoe, much less break the web I've built. I want to thank you for engaging with the program. You brought over seven hundred new cameras online for me. A drop in the bucket compared to the number of cameras world-wide, but I take satisfaction in knowing you'll beat yourself up over all seven hundred day after day."

Kenley grimaced, thankful Savant couldn't see that he was right. "Another few minutes and none of that will matter, Savant. I'll break the web while my friend kills the spider."

Savant's laughter ran a shudder down her spine.

"Why can't we see this guy?" Jude whispered.

"He likes to play games, but he's about to lose this one."

"I always wondered what it was like for a spider to watch its prey struggle in the web before it died. Watching you is giving me an insight into why they leave their victims there for a few days. As you swing in the wind, doing anything to break free and run is delightful to watch, but you may as well stop. You can't go anywhere. It's sad to think you can't run because of the people you've tried to stop all these years. How does it feel, Kenley, to know no matter how hard you try, the bad guys always win?"

"Shoot him. He deserves worse," Kenley growled at Jude, who didn't pull the trigger. She grasped the power cords to reattach to the server. She could almost see the lights flash from yellow to green and back to yellow.

"I wouldn't do that if I were you," a voice said from behind her just as the light in the other office went out.

Jude spun and angled his gun at the voice just as Kenley jammed the cords back into the server. There was a bright flash of light again. That was the last thing Kenley remembered as her world went dark.

Chapter Twenty-One

The monitors beside the bed beeped a steady rhythm, re-assuring Jude more than annoying him. The sound was better than the rapid, irregular and scary rhythm he'd first heard when they got Kenley to the ER. She'd been out cold for hours now, and he was starting to worry that he might never see those sweet brown eyes again. She had to open them soon. He had so much he wanted to share with her about how wonderful their life could be together.

"You've got to wake up, Kenley," he whispered, strok-ing her forehead as the machines clicked and ticked around them. "I've spent my entire life making impossi-ble choices, but this choice, the one I have to make about you, will be the easiest one I've ever made."

"Hey, Jude."

The words brought a smile to his lips, and he leaned forward, surprised to see her eyes open. He expected them to be dull and cloudy, but her brown eyes shone with clar-ity and honesty.

He rubbed her forehead with his thumb in a slow, steady rhythm. "Hey, sweet pea. I've never been happier to see those brown eyes pinned on me."

"What happened?" she asked, her voice hoarse. The

doctors had warned him her voice may come and go for a few days.

"You don't remember?"

Her eyes closed again momentarily, and she took a heavy breath when they reopened. "Savant."

Jude's lips tightened at the name, but he continued to stroke her forehead. "He set you up, sweet pea. We walked right into it."

"All I remember is the bright light in the office and him telling me I would lose." She stopped talking and moved her lips around as though her mouth was parched. He grabbed the cup from the stand and held the straw so she could take a drink. "Thanks. Did you stop him?"

"He was never there, Kenley."

"What? No. He was. We talked to him. He was behind the light, hiding like a coward."

"It was nothing more than smoke and mirrors," he said with a shake of his head. "Cal showed up within seconds of you being electrocuted and cleared the office. There was no one there. He used a spotlight to blind us and was patched into the coms system from somewhere remote."

"Electrocuted?"

Jude nodded as he gazed at the woman he'd fallen head over heels for in a matter of days. "He somehow electrified the server, and when you plugged the cords back in, you took a jolt."

"The server?"

"It was destroyed, but it wasn't the right server. Before he disappeared, he regaled me with the story about how you picked your ego over me, but you fell to his cunningness. Spiderweb remains."

"Electrocuted?" She lifted her hands to her face, turning the white gauze mittens left and right in a dance of disbelief. "My hands!"

"Shh," he soothed her, his heart breaking as a tear leaked from her eye. "It's not as bad as it looks. You have second-degree burns on the palms and several fingers, but they don't think they'll need skin grafts. The dressings will be changed frequently to prevent infection."

"I'll still be able to work?"

"Yes," he promised. "But you'll need some time off to let them heal. We can worry about all of that tomorrow. Today, I want you to rest."

"I didn't pick my ego over you, Jude," Kenley whispered, her eyes fluttering closed for a moment before they snapped open to meet his gaze. "I did it *for* you."

She stressed the word so hard that he tipped his head in confusion. "For me?"

"For the chance to be with you. Our future was too uncertain if I didn't stop Spiderweb from growing. The only way to start a new life with you was to finish my old life and let it disappear. That's what I was trying to do."

"Because if Savant controls all the cameras, he can sell that to the highest bidder, and then we're all at risk?"

Her nod was slight against the pillow with its stark white pillowcase. Her bronze skin was a startling contrast to how full of life she still was just a few hours after nearly dying from electrocution.

"We might be an unconventional couple, but I still wanted a chance to be together," she whispered. "I wanted to experience the kind of love that people talk about, the kind my parents had before they died. I experienced it for the few days we were together, and selfishly, I wanted more. I wanted a life of that kind of love. I love you, Jude Mason.

If I didn't believe in love at first sight, I do now. Maybe I was greedy in doing what I did, but I did it for us, not my ego."

"Shh," Jude whispered, wiping her tears with a tissue from the bedside. "I love you, too, sweet pea. You had me from the moment I heard your voice on the line. When you fell to the floor in that office, I turned my back to a monster to breathe for you until help arrived. I would have traded places with you if I could have, but all I could do was scream for help until Cal pulled me away so the EMTs could take over. I wanted the same chance you did but knew I'd blown it by not insisting we wait for backup."

"No, that was on me," she said with a weak smile. "I should have known Savant would do something dramatic to up the ante. That's how he rolls. He electrified the cabinet on demand?"

"It appears so. The police are still working the scene, but the last I heard, he was able to activate it remotely. The evidence response team said you were lucky. The server below the one you were working on took the biggest hit. You got a residual electrocution, but the one below it would have killed you."

A smile spread across Kenley's face as she lifted her gaze to his. "That's because he didn't want to destroy Spiderweb."

"I don't understand."

The doctors told him she might be confused or even have limited amnesia when she woke up. It appeared they were right, so he reminded himself to be patient with her.

"He wanted me to think the last server, number 7, was his. There was a spiderweb sticker across the front, so all signs pointed to it. He made it too obvious, Jude."

"You were working on the one above it…" The light had come on, and she smiled with a nod.

"I didn't know if that was right, but I took a chance. Did Mina try to get onto the site?"

"No, as soon as they told her you'd been electrocuted, she grabbed an Uber to the hospital. The team just left about an hour ago to head back to Secure Watch."

"Can you text her? Ask her to check the site. See if it loads."

"I will, but you need to rest."

"Once I know," she promised, biting her lip while he texted Mina and waited for her reply. "Savant has a copy of the program somewhere, but he'll have to lay low for a bit now. I hope we bought the government time to get a malware patch in place."

While he waited for Mina to reply, he stroked her forehead and gazed into her tired but bright and alive eyes. "I'll thank God you didn't fall for his ploy every day until I die, Kenley Bates. Everything about you is beautiful, and I want a second chance to protect you for the rest of your life."

"You don't need a second chance. If it weren't for you, I would be God knows where in Savant's lair. This whole thing has taught me the importance of not ignoring our personal safety. I was so focused on my digital safety that I forgot to protect my person, which was my downfall."

His phone beeped, and when he saw the customary greeting, he replied with their question. The response was immediate. "Mina is on it."

Kenley scooted to the edge of the bed. "Lay with me."

She didn't have to ask him twice. He kicked his shoes off and carefully climbed onto the bed, making sure not to jostle any of the wires or tubes that were monitoring the heart and lungs of the woman he loved. Jude just wanted her healthy, and he'd do anything to ensure that happened.

Settled with the blanket over her, he pulled her to him and kissed the top of her head, his eyes going closed as he inhaled the scent of her, even if it was tempered with antiseptic. The phone beeped, and he couldn't help but feel like the next moment would dictate the course of his life from here forward. He lifted it to see a picture response. When he enlarged it, a smile spread across his face. A grim reaper stood against a black screen, a prosthesis on her right leg and a sickle over her shoulder as she was half turned to walk away. Jude showed her the picture, and her giggle of glee healed the fractured portion of his heart to make it whole again.

"I did it," she whispered, relief filling her voice. "Spiderweb is gone. Maybe not for good, but hopefully long enough to find him and destroy the program at its core."

"I love you, sweet pea," he whispered, wrapping his arms around her.

"I love you, too," she said, glancing up into his eyes. "Will you stay with me?"

"I wouldn't be anywhere else," he promised as her lids closed. As he lay there, the truth he had been unable to see all these years was evident. He didn't need to protect all the women in the world; he only needed to protect one. Now that she was in his arms, he was never letting go.

KENLEY EXITED THE conference room, and Jude stood, stretching his hand out for hers. As soon as she was close enough, she slipped hers into his, her soul calm again. It had been two weeks since her showdown with Savant.

The burns on her hands had improved significantly, but she still wore fingerless compression gloves to protect the new skin as it grew in.

"How did it go?" he asked, helping her into his SUV before he jogged around to the driver's side.

"As expected."

"The FBI asked you to work for them?"

Her nod was immediate, but she laughed at the memory. "In at least six different ways and two different languages."

"What did you tell them?"

"No, in two different languages multiple different times."

"You're kidding, right? They didn't ask in two different languages?"

"I'm not kidding." Her laughter filled the car, and he joined in. "They legitimately asked me in English and Spanish—jokingly, I think, after I turned them down in English."

"You didn't have to turn them down on my account," Jude said as he pulled into a spot in front of a pizzeria.

"I didn't turn them down on your account. I turned them down on my account, Jude. I'm done tangling with Savant. He's no longer my problem. If they want to root this guy out of his hole, that's on them. I agreed to help them with situations where my skills can benefit them in exchange for one thing."

"Not working on the task force to find Savant?"

"No." She turned to him and took his hand. "They understood why I didn't want to be on the task force. I agreed to help their coders formulate a camera patch so his program can't control them if he brings it back online."

"Is there a patch that can do that if he's using machine learning?"

"I believe there is. The machine learning aspect has more to do with how the program finds the next camera after one spider is clicked. If we can write a firmware patch for the cameras that confuses the program on where to turn for its next target, eventually it will—" She made a bomb-exploding motion with her hands. "But writing that patch and convincing everyone to install it will take some time. Then again, maybe it won't once Homeland Security contacts the right people. The security world needs to know this was a legitimate threat that is still out there, at least until they can arrest Savant. I got the vibe that they'll do anything to get him into custody, so I suspect it won't be long before that happens."

"Good, he's a dangerous loose end they can't leave hanging. Especially as volatile as he is."

"Agreed. If they can find him, he'll face a whole host of charges, but Savant had nothing to do with my agreement to help them on the dark web. Instead, in exchange for my help, I asked them to investigate Staun Bril Corporation for negligence." Jude's eyes widened, and Kenley grimaced. "Sorry for just dropping that on you, but I didn't know how to tell you I planned to ask them."

"So you just didn't tell me?" Jude asked, clearly hurt. "I'm not sure how I feel about that."

"Don't be upset," Kenley begged. "I was going back and forth on whether I should even ask them. I almost didn't, but when they wanted my help, I decided to go for a give-and-take exchange. Rather than take payment, I want Staun Bril to be investigated. If their crimes are egregious enough, the feds can shut them down."

"If they shut them down, it will be harder to get a settlement, right?"

"Not from what they told me. They said it can go two different ways. They can shut them down and liquidate their assets to pay any lawsuits if they find evidence of negligence. On the other hand, the company can agree to pay any lawsuits, plead guilty to negligence if that can be proven, and remain in business if they fix the problems."

"But it all hinges on proving they're negligent," Jude said, and Kenley nodded. "I promised to give them all the information I have, including access to the forum where all the victims are." She held up her hand. "I'll be transparent about why I'm doing it and move the forum to the World Wide Web where everything is on the up-and-up. That way, anyone on the forum who isn't comfortable talking to the feds doesn't have to join the new forum. It will be a place where anyone else injured by one of their machines can join if a class action lawsuit is filed."

"I must admit, I like the idea of you not being on the dark web where Savant can find you."

"I'll be easier to find on the World Wide Web, but it's riskier for Savant to touch me there. If the FBI has a job for me that I have to work underground, I'll have a new name and persona each time, even if they catch Savant."

"I feel much better about that," he said, kissing her knuckles. "Come on, let's go get dinner. You've had a long day."

She waited for him to come around and open her door, feeling that long day settle into her bones. Her meeting with the government entities had started at 8:00 a.m., and now it was nearly 6:00 p.m. All in all, she was glad it was over. She'd been dreading it since she got out of the hospital and made her way back to her little town house in Milwaukee. Jude had stayed with her, working remotely for Secure Watch from her house while she tried to pick up the pieces of her business part-time while letting her hands heal. Now that this meeting was over, they would have to decide about their future. As Jude opened the door and took her hand, she knew she didn't care what they did as long as they were together.

"I should have asked if you wanted pizza," Jude said as he held the door open for her.

"Pizza is great," Kenley assured him, leaning into his shoulder. "I know you've been craving it since you've been at my place. 'No one makes pizza the way Chicago makes pizza' has never been said more by anyone in the last two weeks." She winked jokingly, and he dropped a kiss on her lips.

"But it's true, though. I'll have to figure out how to get my fix now that I won't live here."

"You're moving?" The surprise had her pulling back on his hand as they entered the restaurant. "You didn't mention that."

"I guess we've both been keeping some secrets from each other," he said, his eyebrow raised. "I'm moving to Minnesota."

Kenley's heart sank, but a familiar voice spoke before she could say more. "It's about time you got here."

"Mina!" Kenley exclaimed, coming face-to-face with the woman who had become a friend over the last few weeks. "I can't believe you're here!"

"We decided it was time to meet the woman who saved the world."

"We saved the world together," Kenley said, her smile bright. "Wait. We?"

"The whole gang," Mina said with a wink.

Kenley threw her arms around Mina and embraced her. "Thank you for everything. For the record, I couldn't have done it without Jude, you and the rest of the team."

Mina motioned them to follow her, and Jude put his hand on Kenley's back as they walked into a small banquet room full of people she'd never met. A giant sign hanging over a buffet table said, WELCOME KENLEY.

"Welcome Kenley?" she asked, turning to Jude, who was grinning like the Cheshire cat as the man she knew as Cal stepped forward.

"It's so good to see you up and moving, Kenley," he said, squeezing her shoulder rather than shaking her hand.

"It's nice to meet you in person finally, Cal. Well, all of you!" The group, which, on quick headcount, was over a dozen people, laughed and nodded as they waved from their positions around the room. Her friend Delilah stepped forward, and Kenley squealed and hurried to her. "You're here!"

"Of course! After all, you did call me. I'd apologize for not answering, but I think things turned out exactly how they were supposed to."

Kenley glanced at Jude, who was still standing in the same place, but all his attention was on her. "I know you're right all the way to my core." After a quick hug, Kenley stepped back and took Delilah's hand. "You look happier than I've ever seen you. I can't wait to catch up and hear all about your honeymoon. First, it seems, we have some pizza to eat."

"Actually," Cal said, motioning to Mina. "We brought you here for a reason."

Mina nodded and motioned at the people standing around the room. Some she'd met, and others she hadn't, but they all wore a Secure Watch or Secure One polo shirt, so she could only assume they all worked together. "I spoke with some of my former colleagues while you were on your way over, and they informed me, much to their chagrin, that you had turned down all of their job offers."

"Yes, ma'am," she said with a nod. "The last thing I want to do is work for the government."

"Good. Then I'm hoping you'll come to work for us," Mina said with a smile.

"I don't know if I'll have time to do contract work along with my business," Kenley said, her heart sinking. Jude said he was moving to Minnesota, and she realized that meant he would be working at Secure Watch.

"She means instead of your business, sweet pea," Jude said from behind her.

When she turned, she nearly ran straight into him. "Like sell my business and work at Secure Watch exclusively?"

"It's not so bad," Cal said, probably hearing the surprise in her voice. "We had five new cabins built on the property this past year. There's room for everyone."

When she glanced back at Jude, he had gotten down on one knee. "I was hoping you might want to share one with me." He pulled out a black box from his pocket and cracked it open. Inside was a teardrop diamond solitaire. "Sorry, sweet pea, it's only a carat," he winked.

Kenley put her hands to her mouth in shock. Was he proposing less than a month from the first time they met? "Are you serious?"

"As I've ever been about anything." He smiled, but she heard the nerves in his voice. "Has it only been three weeks since we met? Yes. Does that matter when I know you're the woman I want to spend the rest of my life with? No. So, I'm down here on one knee asking you to marry me because my gut said you might feel the same way. If you don't want to leave your business, we'll figure it out. All I want is for you to be my wife."

"I put my business up for sale last Friday. I planned to move to Chicago to be closer to you."

"Sounds like you two need to work on communicating better," Lucas said from behind her.

"They were communicating, just not with words," Roman said, dragging groans and laughter from everyone.

Carefully, Kenley knelt and pressed her forehead to Jude's. The laughter and good-natured ribbing around them were drowned out by the beat of their hearts together. "You're sure? You really want to marry the hot mess that is me?"

"Every last burning ember," he answered.

"Then you better put that ring on it and make it official," she said. "Let's make it a short engagement. What's your schedule look like tomorrow?"

His laughter filled her to overflowing as he slid the ring on her finger and planted his lips on hers. Their friends clapped and cheered when he helped her up. When she flashed her finger in the air, the ring twinkled under the lights and threw rainbows across the faces of the people she would now call family.

"It looks like we'll be putting in an application for one of those cabins, Cal," Kenley said as Jude slid his arms around her waist.

"Application accepted and approved!" Cal exclaimed. "Let's eat!" Several servers were loading pizza on the buffet, and with whoops of excitement, everyone streamed toward the table to grab plates of the gooey masterpieces.

Kenley turned in Jude's arms and smiled. "I love you, Mr. Mason."

"Not a smidgen as much as I love you, sweet pea," he whispered, lowering his nose to touch hers. "Are you ready for a fresh start?"

"As long as I'm with you, I'm ready for anything. I couldn't be more excited about a new adventure or living a lighter and happier life with you."

"I'll spend every day from here forward making you happy. I'll start by kissing you right before feeding you a slice of Chicago's best pizza. It's better than wedding cake."

"Well, that's yet to be determined," Kenley whispered. "I'll have to have the wedding cake to make that kind of life decision."

"Set the date, and I'll be there."

"November 21st sounds like the perfect day," she said, leaning closer.

His brow went up as he stared down at her. "That's next week."

"Just enough time to get a license, dress, cake and a justice of the peace. I don't see any reason to wait, do you?"

"Not one," he agreed, lowering his lips to hers. "Tonight, I promise you'll have everything you'll ever want in this life, Kenley Bates."

She had no doubt, because the only thing she'd ever want was him.

* * * * *

Harlequin® Reader Service

Enjoyed your book?

Try the perfect subscription for Romance readers and get more great books like this delivered right to your door.

See why over 10+ million readers have tried Harlequin Reader Service.

Start with a Free Welcome Collection with free books and a gift—valued over $20.

Choose any series in print or ebook. See website for details and order today:

TryReaderService.com/subscriptions